A PHOTO OF MURDER

A SEABREEZE BOOKSHOP COZY MYSTERY BOOK 3

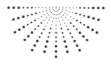

PENNY BROOKE

I saw Marguerite frown at the line of bottles topped by the cardboard faces of a bear, raccoon, and frog.

The supplies for our big event—Martinis in the Garden—had started to come in.

"What exactly, Rue, are we teaching children here?" Marguerite shook her head but not enough to mess with her always-perfect silvery chignon. "Hurl a ball at a sweet-faced frog, and—ding—you get a prize?" She peered more closely at the game, recently delivered by the high school baseball team. "Why, this frog looks like a baby!"

"It's a *ring-toss* game." I waved away her worry. "No frogs—real or fake—will come to any harm at Martinis in the Garden." From my wooden Adirondack chair, I sipped my chardonnay as we watched the sun go down behind the Kingfisher Inn, which Marguerite had run with flair for decades.

By that point in the evening, I had officially turned off the event-coordination portion of my brain. With the spreading golds and purple in the sky, planning had, happily, given way to cocktails.

"Why are there long ears on a *bear?* And that expression on his face…" Marguerite was still hung up on the stupid game. "It gives him the look of a constipated rabbit."

"Well, it was the *baseball* team that contributed the thing, not the art department." I shrugged.

I understood that Marguerite's insistence on perfection had worked well for her. The inn got consistent recognition from prestigious publications all across the country. But perfection had to have its limits. *This was a children's game!*

"Now, if we put *Bill's* picture on those bottles, we could make a fortune, Rue. The whole town would stand in line to knock those suckers down." She gave me a wink, smoothing down the pastel shawl she had artfully draped across one shoulder.

Bill Bright was the former mayor—and not a fan of

change, including our event, which would give a boost to local merchants, many of whom struggled when the tourists left our little piece of heaven by the sea.

"You are just too much," I told Marguerite, amused. I wasn't fooled one bit by the romantic cut of her flowy dress or the careful, tasteful makeup she never went without. Some not-so-demure suggestions could escape those lips, which today were lightly coated in a perfect shade of mauve.

Martinis in the Garden had been my idea to give the Somerset Harbor economy a boost during one of our slower months. A little south of Cape Cod, we saw business swell and ebb as the seasons came and went. While the quiet and cool breezes held a kind of charm that fell over our red-and-gold-burnished falls, charm didn't pay the rent on our expensive storefronts. That included my own baby: the Seabreeze Bookshop.

Bill himself had started an old and tired event aimed at the same problem, but October Days had waned over the years in popularity. It consisted only of a single week of sales with balloons tied to the lampposts and a concert on the square on the final day. Merchants were encouraged to mark down merchandise to get buyers to come out. Evelyn Acato even put a discount on her famous lobster rolls, and those lobster rolls were local treasures, written up *Travel + Leisure* not one time but twice.

Still, fewer and fewer buyers showed up every year. Plus, the whole idea seemed kind of upside down. I was into words, not math, but it made no sense to me: *marking down* top items to *increase* one's bottom line?

So I had suggested something new: a city-wide extravaganza to be held in local gardens. Some of the gardens here were beyond magnificent. Plus, the cooler weather and sea breezes made afternoons and early evenings in October almost magical—a great time to be out. We could invite local merchants to set out their food and wares, string tiny lights among the trees, and have soft music playing, thanks to a local harpist and our string quartet.

I had recruited Marguerite to help me with the cause, and she had eagerly jumped in. She didn't have that title I was saddled with: *outsider.* Here among the old families of the Harbor, ten years—or even fifteen—meant "new kids on the block." Less than a year like me, and forget about it. It barely seemed to matter that my gran had run the store before me. I wasn't Gran, you see.

My first act of "rebellion" had been to paint the bench beside my walkway a very tasteful blue. I'd added a small table so a customer might enjoy a slice of fudge or a cup of coffee while he dived into his books.

The verdict had come in swiftly from a string of guests.

"This simply isn't done." Bill Bright had screwed up his face, as if the fish had just turned rancid in his bouillabaisse from Laurinda's Grab and Go.

Beth Arrington, head of standards and compliance for the merchants group, had been next.

"There was no application made and no approval given," she'd pronounced with a sigh.

"Approval? I don't get it." I'd been beyond confused. "It's my bench that I paid for, and it's sitting at *my* store."

"Convenient for your customers with the little table there. A nice addition, Rue, *but blue?*" asked the police chief, who had hurried over, seemingly to investigate *the color of a bench.* Or maybe he'd just heard the new Michael Connelly book had finally come in. (I hoped that was the case.)

My new addition didn't fit, it seemed, with the upscale, understated feel of the downtown area, whose colors seemed to be dark beige, barely beige, and tan.

All of this to say it was because of Marguerite May, respected citizen and a member of the "club," that a buzz of excitement had begun about Martinis in the Garden —much to Bill's chagrin.

"Rue, I do believe our extravaganza will be *beyond exquisite,*" she told me now with a smile. "With little twinkling lights blinking in the trees, will it not be *enchanting?* Oh! And Arianna Lee will be bringing china from her resale shop—for serving tea and treats. The whole mixing-and-matching-patterns thing is so on trend these days." She smiled, pleased with her idea. "It will give the whole thing a very classy, tea-party kind of feel."

"What a fun idea." If impractical.

"The young people of today, from what I understand, have no use for fine china. Way too busy they are! Something delicate and fine has no place in their world."

At sixty-seven, Marguerite was old-school and proud of it.

"Speaking of mix and match, do you think our choice of food is…kind of a weird fit for Arianna's fancy plates?" I made a mental list of the restaurants who'd committed to Martinis in the Garden. "Deep-fried Oreos and slaw dogs served on fine bone china?"

Marguerite threw back her head and laughed, a deep and throaty sound that was full of joy. "The china's only for a few of the fancier desserts. And, of course, for tea. Otherwise, we'd be handwashing till the tourists all returned."

I closed my eyes against the breeze, savoring the notes of plum and apple in the chardonnay; only the finest food and drinks were served at the Kingfisher Inn, which was one of the historic landmarks that helped lure tourists from Cade Cod to our midsize town. A who's who of authors, politicians, and directors had stayed on the premises, and their pictures lined the halls. To add to its prestige, the inn was one of the few remaining homes designed by the celebrated Armory Beaumont. It was said to have been intended for his daughter, who tragically died young in a sailing accident. Now, it sprawled majestically behind us with its high-pitched roofs, array of balconies, and meticulous grounds and gardens.

I reached for an oatmeal cookie from the plate of assorted treats Marguerite had set between us. That's when something tickly brushed against my feet.

"What the..." I startled, looking down. The striped cat who "ran" the inn with Marguerite was halfway across the yard, a blur of gray and brown. "What is up with Beasley?" I pressed my hand to my chest to still my thumping heart.

"Restless energy? Who knows? He just does that sometimes." Marguerite reached for one of her famous cheese straws and gave me a knowing look. "Now, if I was not a woman of intelligence and sense, I'd say he'd seen *the ghost.*"

Marguerite did not believe for one second in the ghost of a young woman who had, the story goes, flung herself off a balcony at some point in the history of the Kingfisher Inn. "Stuff and utter nonsense," Marguerite had told me on numerous occasions. She would much prefer the bloggers and reporters put their focus on the history of the house, which she had furnished with antiques, many of them from the time in which the building was constructed and served as a private home.

Or she would have preferred the focus be on the sheer amazingness that came out of her kitchen. Marguerite May was a master cook, making use of fresh local seafood as well as herbs from the two gardens at the inn. Treats were always set out, and breakfast was a feast: apple-stuffed French toast, crème brûlée with bacon and brown sugar, pomegranate cream cheese muffins; the list went on and on.

Like the furniture, many of her recipes had come down from a previous owner of the property. Marguerite's ties to the area were that long and deep.

Yet the stories of the ghost had been persistent through the years. Guests swore up and down the doors to their balconies swung open in the night. Distant wails were frequently reported. There might be whispers over breakfast of a pale figure who was seen fleeing through the gardens in a long white dress.

Marguerite recounted a few of the ghostly tales as she slowly sipped her second glass of chardonnay. One family insisted they were followed by a "moist and chilly mass, a kind of eerie presence" even as a record heat wave overtook the town a few summers back. "*A moist and chilly mass?*" Marguerite let out a snort. "That sounds more disgusting than ghostly or romantic."

Ghostly and romantic often was the draw for guests at the Kingfisher Inn. In fact, even as we spoke, among that week's occupants were the cast and crew of *Is My House Really Haunted?* That included Max Dakota, the wacky, wild-haired host of the top-rated show on the Worst Nightmares Network. (Catchphrase: "Do you Dare to Watch?")

"How goes it with the TV crew?" I reached for a key lime cookie. I'd watched a few groups of lookie-loos pass by *very slowly,* hoping for a glimpse of Max.

Marguerite rolled her eyes. "Max Dakota! What a piece of work. Two weeks before he checked in, his people called the inn with a list of his demands: organic fruit juice in his room, a pair of sleeping pants, Disney theme preferred. This man's top dresser drawer was to be filled with—are you ready?—Skittles, Sour Patch Kids, and dark chocolate. With nuts but not pecans. Who does he think he is, Beyoncé?"

I laughed. "Disney pants and Skittles. Not such a

spooky guy." I drew out all the *o's* in "spooky" like in the intro to the show: *And now here is Max Dakota, such a spooooky guy!*

"I told his handlers to shove it. I figured he needed me and the Kingfisher ghost as much as I needed him."

"Good for you," I said.

"My ghost is a primo ghost—deluxe. They'll tune in droves to check out *my* ghost, as Max is well aware."

Privately, Marguerite called all of it absurd. But publicly, she sold books on *Haunted Massachusetts* at the front desk. She'd compiled a cookbook to set out on the shelves: *Ghostly Treats to Die for from the Kingfisher Inn.* In other words, she took the money. She *was* a business-woman, and even the stately Kingfisher had its share of months when finances were tight.

The most sought-after souvenir was the T-shirt that proclaimed "I Slept in Room 282 at the Kingfisher Inn." On the back, it read "And I Lived to Check Out."

The legend of the ghost had somehow become attached to that specific room. And those with the luck —or courage—to have secured a reservation were part of a special club, which had its own "282 Survivors" page on Facebook. There was a Twitter hashtag and meetups across the country. (Receipt required to prove your stay in the favorite room of the Kingfisher ghost.)

I thought back to the cat and his mad dash. "So Beasley's a believer in your famous spirit?"

"It looked like it for a moment." A faraway look passed across the eyes of my hostess. "And perhaps he has a point."

I studied her intently. "No way, Marguerite. Are you going soft on me? Of all the people in the world, I can't believe that *you* would ever entertain the notion of a ghost. After all these years!"

She gave me a wry smile. "Well, I'm not ready to pour salt on all the doorways yet. Or to fill up the place with vases of white roses as Max has recommended. That will supposedly suck up all activities of a paranormal nature. The kind of things you learn when ghost hunters come to town!" She smiled. "Of course, I've promised not to do anything at all until he gets the 'ghost' on film. If the ghost checks out, that means no show for Max." She paused. "Of course, he also says the first thing I should do is ask myself some questions: Does this ghost *need* to go? Are her intentions good—or evil?"

I let that idea sink in. "*A ghost of good intentions*—I would say she is. A sad ghost, from what I've heard, but nothing mean about her. I vote you let her stay," I teased.

"Oh, she's not going anywhere. I need her to pay my bills."

The conversation hit a lull, both of us lost in thought. Then Marguerite broke the silence. "Between you and me, my dear," she told me quietly, "I myself have felt a...*presence* in the last few weeks."

I gave her a look that indicated my surprise.

"This must seem like crazy talk, like I've been spending too much time with that awful Max Dakota." She stared straight ahead at a cherry tree whose flowers had somehow managed to hold on this late in the season. "But I mean *regrets,* not ghosts. Spirits from my past who have come back to remind me that I have... caused a lot of hurt." She stared into the setting sun. "Forgetting is a solace, Rue, I do not deserve."

"Oh, that can't be true, I'm sure." For me and many others, Marguerite had gracefully stepped in to take the place of no-show volunteers, speak her mind to bullies, and anonymously make payments on the delinquent bills of others. "I don't know what you've done wrong, but I know what you've done right."

She gazed ruefully at the now empty bottle and gave me a sad smile. "We have hit upon a very foolish combo: an old lady and her memories and too much Domaine Chenevieres Chablis."

She shook her head as if to shake bad thoughts away.

"We all have regrets," I said.

"Or perhaps I've conjured up the spirit of my

younger self—who I have decidedly let down. And to tell the truth, I'll bet she's angry with me too." She set down her glass. "Oh. Listen to me ramble! But when you're old, you see, your mind just roams and roams—and sometimes takes you back to places you never wished to see again." She paused. "So much was lost. So foolish."

I was surprised to see tears standing in her eyes.

"Do you want to talk about it?" I asked in part because I was desperate to help. And also, I admit, because I was curious. I was, after all, a connoisseur of stories—and now I sensed a story that had waited a long time to be told.

"Oh, Rue, I'll be just fine, and I need to get inside and set out some evening snacks." A look of worry crossed her eyes. "Did you see where Beasley got to?"

As if he'd been summoned, the cat leaped into her lap.

Marguerite scratched his back. "This little one has had it rough this week. He's sensitive, my baby, to a lot of noise, and Max Dakota is *so loud.* The man's voice can really carry, and his crew goes around with all of this *equipment* that beeps and whirs and such."

"That sounds like a mess."

"But not every little thing is doom and gloom with me. I may have good news soon." Her blue eyes took on a girlish sparkle.

"Do I get a hint?"

"Oh, let me think about it." She gave me a wink. "I think it will surprise you, and it's…well, it's rather nice. That's all you get for now. But when we meet on Tuesday to go over the spreadsheet for the event, you'll get hint number two."

"Well, aren't you the tease?" I laughed.

The thing about it, though, was I never got that hint.

The next morning as I unpacked boxes of new books, I was surprised to see my business partner enter. Elizabeth wasn't scheduled till the afternoon.

"Rue." She paused and stared. Her long curls were a mess, tangled and knotted down her back, and her face was ashen.

"Elizabeth! You're early." My heart was in my throat; her look told me right away that she had news—and that her news would crush me like a vise.

She walked a little closer, then she stopped, as if the words were just too ugly to let out into the room. Then she took a breath. "I wanted you to know, to hear it from me first, before you overheard it from some gossip. The way this town loves to talk…"

"Elizabeth, just say it." She was my best friend and I

loved her, but she could drag things out, and this was not the time. She had to say it. Now.

"Rue, it's Marguerite. They found her this morning at the inn." The last part came in an almost whisper. "Marguerite is gone."

A chill shot through my chest. "But just last night I saw her! That cannot be right." I forced myself to breathe. "Was it her heart, Elizabeth? Do they know what happened?" I sank down onto the stool behind the register.

"It was not her heart, Rue." My best friend's voice was gentle. "Marguerite was strangled."

"*What?*" There was no way. "But who would…who would do that to Marguerite and *why?*" The whole thing seemed unreal.

"Now, that I do not know. I heard from Lily down the street they used one of her scarves to do it, the kind she always likes to wear."

"The spirits," I said softly. "She had felt the presence of some spirits." Had the spirits come to warn her? Had she somehow sensed *this horror* on the way?

Elizabeth looked at me, concerned. "Now you're not talking sense. I don't think you're well, which is understandable right now."

I was still lost in thought. The talk the night before was all coincidence, I assured myself. It was talk about *the past,* and regrets don't up and strangle you with silky Yves Laurent.

My golden retriever lumbered over and lay his head on my lap. Gatsby always got me. "Good boy," I whispered as I rubbed behind his ears. "What happened to her, Gatsby?"

CHAPTER TWO

*W*hen I got myself together, Elizabeth had quietly begun to unpack the new merchandise. Only one customer was in, browsing in self-help.

"Rue, you should be home." Elizabeth picked up another box. "Go on home. I've got this."

"Do they know what time it happened?" I was still full of questions. Had someone been there waiting even as we sat outside with our chardonnay? My chest was in knots.

"I have no idea. She was discovered by a maid," Elizabeth told me gently. "It happened in *that room*—the one they say is haunted."

"Please tell me they have leads. Do they know, Elizabeth, who might have done a thing like that? Oh shoot; I've asked you that already. I'm just...not myself."

"Well, of course you're not." She put a hand on my shoulder. "Take some time today. I need to be here anyway to work on the exhibit. I'll get these books unpacked, and I can handle customers and go through photos in between."

In conjunction with Martinis in the Garden, Elizabeth was curating an exhibit of old photos: "Somerset Harbor Families Through the Years." Many of the photos would be pulled from her corner of the shop, Antiquities by Elizabeth. It featured postcards, photos, books, and more for vintage treasure hunters.

"Thank you. That sounds great. But let me slip back to my office first and see what Andy knows." My oldest friend in town worked as a PI and was in the know when it came to local crime. Once a top police investigator, he'd grown tired of the department's inefficiency and gone to work for himself. But the chief still called him in for the bigger cases. They needed Andy on the big ones; Andy knew his stuff.

He answered on the first ring. "Hey, Rue. I know you have a million questions, but I'll have to call you back. Things are crazy here." In the background I heard shouting.

"Are you at the inn?"

"Me and the whole force. A lot to process here." Andy lowered his voice. "Did you know that haunted house show is filming here in town?"

Everyone but Andy knew that, I was sure. He was too engrossed in his crossword puzzles and classic Western shows to listen to town gossip.

"Just two questions, Andy, and I will let you go. Who killed Marguerite and why? What is your best guess?"

"Unknown at this time—which is why I have to go. Also, there's this weird dude who just strolled into the lobby and might be about to blow. Guy is dressed up like a clown. I swear! Hair sprouting up in all directions, shouting things that make no sense."

"He's not about to blow. That is how he always acts—on TV anyway. That is Max Dakota from that show, *Is My House Really Haunted?*" I leaned back in my desk chair. "So, no clue about the reason..." I almost couldn't say it. "Why Marguerite was killed?"

He lowered his voice. "I'll come right out and say it so I can get to work; you *are* persistent, Rue. We think some of her...um, her ways of doing business may have...strayed a little bit from the up and up. What we might be looking at is an act of revenge."

I held in a gasp. "That can't possibly be true."

"Just a theory, Rue."

"And you think this because..."

He sighed. "Rue, don't you understand I'm standing in the middle of a crime scene and I need to get to work?"

"Well, how long until you're free?" My heart was racing now. "I'll come and meet you there...because, Andy, we should talk." I should let him know for sure what Marguerite had said: *I have caused a lot of hurt.* It could be related to this talk of business fraud, as nonsensical and unlike Marguerite that theory seemed to be.

But then again, the things that caused her anguish seemed way back in her past. *When you're old, you see, your mind just roams and roams—and sometimes takes you back to places you never wished to see again.*

I heard Andy confer with someone about "chain of evidence" and "just two more seconds." Then he got back to me. "You have no business here, Rue. *Do not come to the scene.* I will call you when I can."

In the background I heard banging, the murmurs of a crowd, and, above it all the distinct incantations of the most famous ghost hunter of them all. "Spirit, are you there?" A loud beep followed that and then the voice of Bob Lee, the chief of police. "Sir, we have warned you once. You must cease and desist."

Then I remembered Beasley and his fear of loud noises. Marguerite's furry child! Now, in addition to the ghost-detection stuff that beeped and buzzed and whirred, there were swarms of cops added to the mix.

"Andy! Do you have the cat?"

"*What*? You know I'm allergic, Rue. Why would I have *a cat*? Look, I really have to go."

"I'm coming for the cat!" He must be terrified.

"The cat? What cat? Did you say you're coming *here*? Rue, I must insist…"

"See you in a sec."

Max Dakota was standing in a sea of blue uniforms, camera operators, and technical equipment. Holding a bright red phone—an old-fashioned landline of all things—he was shouting into the receiver. "Spirit, are you there?"

Like a good television fan, I already knew the answer. The spirit always rang every Friday night between eight and nine—despite the fact that the stupid phone was not plugged into a wall.

In addition to the phone, Max also came equipped with what he claimed to be the latest in ghost-hunting gear. With his state-of-the-art equipment, he and his team located ghostly cold spots. They recorded sounds "from the other side" that were barely audible to the unaided ear. And they took shockingly realistic photos of otherworldly-looking apparitions. But after all the fancy toys had done their fancy things, the ghost called to tell its story on an old-fashioned landline.

The red phone, Max explained, had now become well known in the "community of spirits." In other words, the ghosts had told their ghost friends they could tell their tragic stories to the world via Max Dakota. Then they could move on to the spirit realm—and the fans and sponsors could go wild.

Now, Max looked into the camera as he spoke. "In an unprecedented episode in the history of our series, we will feature interviews with the proprietress of the Kingfisher Inn, who was brutally strangled last night with a silk scarf, taking her last breath near this very spot."

A crowd was looking on, including several officers, their arms crossed in front of them, perturbed expressions on their faces.

Max continued with his spiel. "I arrived at the Kingfisher with my team to track down a single ghost—but now there may be two!" His brown eyes pierced the camera. "I anticipate that Marguerite will appear not only as a live guest but as a spirit too—to describe for us what happened. From. Beyond. The grave." His voice boomed across the room.

Fury overtook me. How exploitive could he get? I looked around for Marguerite's assistant Heather, who I guessed was in charge. She should kick this joker out.

Okay Rue, just breathe. You have a cat to catch.

An older handsome man was standing in the corner. Something in his eyes made him appear to be approachable and kind.

"Excuse me, sir, have you seen a gray striped cat? He could be in here somewhere, or he may have run outside. You never really know. He's *somewhere* on the property. I hope!"

"Oh, you must mean Beasley." The older gentleman let out a sigh. "I forgot about the cat. And no, I'm afraid I haven't seen the little guy. He must be really hating all of this commotion." Then he closed his eyes, obviously overcome. "Marguerite would tell us we were being derelict. I can hear her now, saying *Someone catch that cat.*"

I looked at him with interest. He was tall with finely chiseled features, salt and pepper hair, an expensive-looking, well-pressed button-down.

"You must have been staying here a while," I said. He seemed to know Marguerite—and Beasley—well.

"Joe Ripley." He held out a hand. "In town from New York."

"I'm Rue." I hesitated. "So, are you hearing anything?

About a suspect or a motive? I just can't imagine. This is so unreal."

"Unbelievable."

I could almost swear his eyes were a little wet.

"I have been here watching," he continued, "hoping to learn more. I have often found the most expedient pathway to information is to keep my mouth shut and let others talk." He folded his arms across his chest, still studying the scene. "The police, it seems, are looking for an unknown woman who was recently at the inn."

Very interesting. "Do you know any more?"

"Well, I did let them know of a young lady who might be worth a look. One of my fellow guests." He looked around the room. "I don't see her now. And it may be another woman altogether they are looking for. It seems they have some kind of lead."

"Why do you think the other guest might have been involved?"

A hard look flashed across his eyes. "She was cold to Marguerite, this young woman was, like she had an ax to grind. Marguerite, of course, was nothing but a gracious host, and this girl couldn't seem to spare so much as a smile or thank you. And then—it was two days ago I think—she and Marguerite seemed to be having words. I started to step in, but then things seemed to settle, so I let it go."

26

I noticed we were near the wall of famous guests and pictures that detailed the history of the building and the town. I found Marguerite in several pictures and locked on to her smile for comfort.

At the top of the display, a young girl in a formal portrait looked out upon the scene. Some claimed she was the daughter of the home's architect, the girl who had died so tragically before she could move in. Some claimed this was a portrait of the famous ghost herself as she had appeared in life. The picture had been featured in several magazines covering the famous hauntings. Its place—dead center in the top row—gave it an important air, as did its ornate frame.

Of course, I'd asked Marguerite about the picture.

"A lot of these people's stories are unknown, which is excellent for business," she had said. "Guests and journalists, you know, just adore a mystery."

The picture was undated, but the cloche-style hat atop the woman's curls hinted that the picture might date back to the thirties. There was a gleam in the woman's eyes and just the trace of a smile, as if she were amused at all the people and their theories about who she was.

From across the room, I noticed Andy watching me. I said goodbye to Joe and headed over.

My detective friend pulled me into a laundry room

away from listening ears. His white shirt strained against his wide girth as he pulled out a handkerchief to mop sweat from his brow.

I got right to business since he was in a rush. "Unknown woman. Who is she?"

"So, you've been investigating. Why am I not surprised?" He sighed. "We don't know a lot. But she was seen with Marguerite last night. From what we understand, their conversation got intense."

"Was she young?" I thought about the woman Joe had described.

"Witnesses were under the belief she was in her thirties. Attractive and well-dressed. She and Marguerite, as I understand it, sat outside the inn and talked for quite a while. Talked and drank some wine."

It was my turn to sigh. "Andy, she's right here. The unknown woman's here." Unknown and *attractive;* at least there was that, and I guess my comfy wrap dress was more stylish than I thought. *Well-dressed,* he had said.

Andy grabbed my arm. "Rue, do you know this woman? Tell me where she is!"

"She's in the laundry room." I leaned back against a dryer with my eyebrow raised.

Andy wildly looked around. For a smart detective, he could sometimes be clueless.

"Andy! You don't get it. The unknown woman's me."

"Wait a minute. *What?*"

"Martinis in the Garden! You know that I'm in charge with Marguerite. We had a planning meeting, which evolved into a glass of wine—well, *one glass of wine* with refills. And lots of conversation."

"Well, why did you not say?" His face collapsed.

"If you hadn't rushed me off the phone, I would have told you then—but it's not exactly like she told me anything you would need to know...exactly."

"We're still gonna need to get a statement from you. Let me inform Bob Lee." He looked down at his two-way radio.

"But first, I am the one who will need some information—cause this is killing me. What's up with this talk of fraud? You surely don't believe it."

"Rue, I'm really hoping that it isn't true—but life can send some shockers flying at you when you least expect it. I see it all the time in the business that I'm in."

"You have evidence?" I asked.

"Just suspicions at this point. It could be really nothing, just one of several leads." He touched my arm. "I'm really sorry, Rue. I know you two had gotten close."

"Give me details, Andy. You know that I need details."

"Let's just say for now a fight was overheard and

there were accusations. The person spoke of 'theft' and 'abuse of trust,'" he continued quietly. "Those specific words were used. But I've probably said too much, so I'm gonna shut my mouth for now."

A knot formed in my chest. "Well, I would tend, of course, to believe Marguerite and not some unnamed accuser." My anger was boiling up again.

"But there was something else."

The knot tightened in my chest.

Andy continued, "Someone from the cleaning staff said she heard Marguerite call Beckham Properties last week. She was asking how much time it would take the inn to sell if she put it on the market now."

That was a surprise, but still… "That is hardly cause for these kinds of accusations. It would be her right to sell the Kingfisher and retire."

"It's just how she went about it, so hush-hush and all of that." He mopped his brow again. "None of her closest friends seemed to have an inkling she might be thinking of a change. Apparently, she indicated on the call she might be moving out of state. 'The sooner the better,' is what she told the agent on the phone. Consistent with the activities of someone who might feel the need to flee."

"Ridiculous." I shook my head at him. "You said you have other leads?"

"There is some jewelry we've determined to be missing. Very pricey pieces, so there's that. Theft could be a motive. The extent of items missing has yet to be determined, but Bob seems to be more focused on this other theory—the killer having acted in revenge over some type of fraud or deception."

"You can't let this get out." I looked into Andy's eyes. "Let her have her dignity. Because you and I both know this fraud thing is absurd. It's too unlike her, Andy. You know Marguerite! She wouldn't hurt a...cardboard frog."

He frowned at that last remark then put an arm around me. "Oh, Rue," he told me softly, "what a day it's been."

I was filled with thankfulness for Andy's presence on the case. He'd always been the sane voice when Bob Lee would take off on some misdirected path, anxious to secure his reputation for wrapping cases quickly. (Maybe incorrectly, but quickly just the same.)

I vowed in that moment to keep a close eye on the case. I had Marguerite's good name to protect. And I was positioned well to hear little tidbits that could prove to be important. Booksellers were a lot like bartenders in that way. My customers, you see, not only *purchased* stories; they were always full of real-life stories from the town. The tea station at the register was my subtle way of saying "Linger for a while." My customers were friends.

"Listen, Rue, I might as well get that statement from you now about your visit here with Marguerite last night." Andy pulled a notebook from his pocket.

Then we were startled by the sound of footsteps rushing past. Both of us turned to see Max Dakota charging down the hall with his team close behind, their arms full of things that lit up and beeped. When he reached the laundry room, Max paused. He waved his hands in the air and began to chant as I traded looks with Andy.

A camera operator moved very close to Max as the TV host exclaimed, "I felt her here. Just now! Ladies and gentlemen, Marguerite May has yet to depart from the Kingfisher Inn." He held up what I recognized to be Marguerite's favorite brooch: two diamond-encrusted ruby hearts intertwined with one another. "She has left this sign for me that she is with us still," Max said.

Andy then sprung forward and grabbed Max by the arm. "I believe that is *my* sign you need to come with me. That is stolen jewelry you have there."

"What an outrage!" Max exclaimed. "Do you know who I am?" He turned to his cameramen, who were scrambling behind him. "Are you getting this on film? So that the world can watch this man interfering with my process, which is *very delicate.*" Then his voice grew more excited. "Film that!" he exclaimed.

I followed his eyes. Was he pointing to…my leg?

Looking down, I jumped. A stack of folded sheets on a low shelf to my left had begun to slowly move.

"Another spirit has made contact!" Max yelled over his shoulder as Andy dragged him down the hall. "What message does it have for all of us today?"

I looked back at the shelf. The sheets were drifting toward me. Okay, this was weird. Panic seized my chest as I froze in place. What had Marguerite been saying yesterday about how to lose a ghost?

Wait! What was I even thinking? *I did not believe in ghosts.*

Still, I backed away—until a small gray head peeked out from underneath the sheets. Beasley was all eyes; they were huge and terrified.

"There you are." I snatched him up. "You can come with me for now."

CHAPTER THREE

"I see you've brought a friend." From her table in the corner, Elizabeth glanced up from a line of photographs.

"Until further notice, we have a second cat." I set Beasley down.

Cautiously, he crept toward a display of bookmarks, giving them a sniff.

"Hey Beasley!" said Elizabeth. "Bet you'd like some water." She stood up and headed to the sink in back.

Gatsby, ever friendly, barked happily in greeting.

Cat number one, our tiny ball of white fluff, looked a little miffed as he snuggled up to the new releases. Oliver intently studied the newcomer.

Elizabeth put some water down for Beasley and brought me some tea. Gratefully I took a sip as I settled into one of the comfy chairs next to the register. "Perfect," I pronounced. "This one is delicious."

"Honey lavender. They say it's good for stress." Elizabeth lowered herself into the chair across from me. "I thought you were taking the day off."

"I didn't want to be alone." I gave her the updates from the inn and also told her about my talk the night before with a troubled Marguerite. I leaned back against the chair and closed my eyes, so tired. "I need to figure out what the heck is going on."

She raised an eyebrow at me. "Or the police could do it. They're trained for that, you know."

"Well, it seems to me the chief is stuck on this idea of fraud. If they concentrate on that, then word will get around, and I just can't stand for Marguerite to get talked about like that."

Elizabeth glanced over at her table. "I've been isolating photos that feature Marguerite. I thought it might be nice to highlight some of those as part of the exhibit. It could be a kind of tribute to her since she planned the event. I've found a few when she was young, but we don't really know a lot about her family. You know, for the theme: 'Families Through the Years.'"

That would have to be mother, father, siblings, since Marguerite had never had a husband or children of her own.

"That's a really nice idea," I said.

Oliver jumped into my lap, maybe to remind me he was my cat first before the "interloper" showed.

"So, what's new with you?" I asked, needing a distraction from the talk of murder.

"Well, I've spent time sorting photos." Elizabeth stood up to fix some tea for herself. "It was quite the morning. I helped some customers, I unpacked some books—and Rue, you won't believe it; Rue, I fell in love."

That made zero sense. "You fell in love *this morning*? I don't understand. Tell me right this instant."

Elizabeth was not one to exaggerate or talk about her love life—or to *have* a love life even. Let's just say her luck was bad when it came to romance, more *Bridget Jones* with a trace of *Gone Girl* than a Shakespeare sonnet.

"Let me introduce you." She gave me a wink as she headed to her table, and soon she was handing me a photo.

I studied it. "Oh my."

A man, who appeared to be somewhere in his twenties, leaned against a Porsche and laughed at whoever held the camera. Strands of dark silky curls were blowing in his face. His blue eyes were intense, and the muscles in his arms strained against the rolled-up sleeves of his crisp white shirt. But it was the man's smile that made me very sure I would have liked this guy.

"Who is this?" I asked.

"Oh, I have no idea."

"Serious stumbling block in this romance of yours."

"And also there is this." She pointed to the date on the white edge of the photo: 1970. "Leave it to me to fall in love with some guy who's either dead or really, really old."

The tinkling of a bell announced a customer. "Well, let me get to work." I stood, handing her back her vintage beau.

"Can I help you?" I asked the young woman. Her blonde hair was pulled back into a ponytail from which one small curl escaped. She looked a little lost or maybe fearful.

Beasley peered from behind a shelf and stared, then he zoomed off to the back at lightning speed.

"Sorry, brand-new cat," I said to the customer. "He's still getting used to us. What can I help you find?"

She spoke in a quiet, formal voice. "Twentieth-century antiques? Might you have some books on that?" She spoke almost in a whisper.

"I believe you are in luck. Let me take you to the section on collectibles and hobbies." I led her toward the back. "You look familiar to me," I told her as we walked. Her thin white gauzy dress seemed to almost swallow her thin frame, swishing around her ankles as she moved. "Do you live here in town?" I asked.

"I don't."

Okay, so not the chatty type.

I left her alone to browse. I'd found some customers preferred to be alone as they dipped into the worlds between the pages, deciding which of them they wanted to take home. And then some customers were simply in a mood. I suspected that was true of this one, whose eyes were red and puffy, her complexion drained of color.

Elizabeth, back to working at her table, must have noticed too. "Tea?" she asked the woman. "We have some lovely flavors. So nice on a cool day, and it's on the house this afternoon."

At least this time the woman managed a hint of a smile when she said, "No, thank you."

I unpacked part of another box while the woman looked around, then she approached the desk with two books to purchase: *Heirlooms and Other Treasures* and *A Companion for Collectors.*

"I do hope you enjoy these." I slipped them into a bag.

She simply nodded and was off.

"She seemed really sad," Elizabeth remarked once the door had shut behind the customer.

"Well, this is a sad day." I went back to my unpacking. "She looked familiar to me."

"Yes!" Elizabeth crinkled up her forehead. "I was thinking the same thing." She picked up a photo, continuing her work. "Quite a reaction there from Beasley. I guess we need to train him on the etiquette of greeting customers."

"He did that same thing last night. Marguerite was saying it was like he saw the ghost."

The Ghost.

In my mind I saw the portrait of the woman at the inn. *That is where I'd seen her.* The customer had those same eyes, the same face. It was like I had been looking at the portrait come to life in modern clothes. Of course, it wasn't her. That woman was long dead, but still…

"Elizabeth!" I said. "You will not believe what I just figured out. That woman looked exactly—"

I was interrupted with a gasp from Elizabeth. "*Now* I understand why she looks familiar, Rue. You have to see this photo I just came across today. Come! You have to look. It's uncanny, Rue."

I hurried to take the photo she was holding out to me. A family group was gathered around a picnic basket, scattered toys, and half-empty plates. The four adults looked solemn while four little girls were a whirl of giggles, waves, and movement.

In the center of it all *seemed* to be the young lover of antiques who had just left my store. Except it couldn't be. The older-model car behind the group and the wide skirts spread around the women marked this as a time long ago and far away.

"A photo from the fifties." Elizabeth read my mind.

But it looks exactly like her. I stared at the picture. I tried to dispel the weirdness with a joke. "So what is she, a ghost?" I gave Elizabeth a half smile. "She did look super pale," I said as I felt a little shiver—despite the fact I most emphatically *did not believe in ghosts.*

"Came back to mourn her daughters, I suppose." Elizabeth turned the photo over. In cursive were some words that ripped my heart in two: "RIP Patricia 1949-1954, Dorothy 1951-1954, and Susan 1946-1954." A trio of angel stickers was lined up beneath.

I looked once more at the picture, which somebody had blown up to a five-by-seven. One of the little girls hugged her sister from the back while another held her doll up to display for the camera. One held her mouth wide open, her eyes squeezed in delight, as if she were in the middle of a funny tale. Also in the photo were an older couple and a man in a felt fedora.

"Okay, this breaks my heart," I said. "What happened to the girls? And *who are these people?*"

"I have no idea about the girls." Elizabeth leaned back in her chair and pulled her hair over one shoulder. "At first I thought these might be relatives of Marguerite. I've been on a push, you know, to find some family pictures to put up in her honor—for the 'family photo' theme." She looked down at a stack of photos on her desk. "Although we could go with photos from the inn if that's what we have to do—all the famous guests she's met."

I sat down in the folding chair she kept near her table. "Why did you think these people might have been related to her?" I put the photo down and pushed it toward Elizabeth.

"Because of this man here." She pointed to the young man in the photo. "By the name of Thomas Perkins. The daughter who survived—Henrietta was her name—appeared in some later photos side by side with Marguerite. So I was pulling all the photos I could find of the family, who ran a five and dime for years on the south side of town.

Elizabeth was a kind of walking history book when it came to our town.

"His name was on an envelope that held just this picture and a paper valentine, the kind little kids give out." She looked down at the photo. "It was part of a lot of papers, letters, and the like." She sighed. "But the obituary was online today, and it turns out Marguerite was an only child. No mention of anyone named Perkins in her family history. And there were no survivors listed by that name."

"So I guess Henrietta Perkins was just a friend of Marguerite's," I said. "Except…"

After a pause, Elizabeth looked at me expectantly.

"You are going to think that I've lost my mind."

"Oh, I've known that for a while," she teased. Then she turned serious. "What are you thinking, Rue?"

"Today I looked again at that famous picture, the one some journalists and websites think might be the ghost. That last customer who came in looked *so much* like the picture that I can hardly breathe—*and* so much like your photo."

I was overcome by everything: the brutal strangling of a friend, the crazy fact that *some kind of apparition* seemed to have drifted into my store and put two books on her AmEx.

Elizabeth grabbed my hand. "All of this is too much, Rue. You need to go home and lie down."

Gatsby, who could always sense my pain, began to whimper and lay down by my feet. On my other side,

Oliver snuggled against my ankle. Together the two of them formed a warm and furry nest of comfort.

Elizabeth leaned toward me. "Let me stick a pin in whatever crazy notion you have lodged inside your head. The woman in this photo, Thomas Perkins's wife, *could not* have been a guest at the Kingfisher Inn—because she was a local. So no way is she the ghost."

"No matter where she lived, she could have still walked in, gone up to the second floor, and flung herself off that balcony, as the story goes." I gazed down at the photo. "After burying three daughters in a single year, it would make a kind of sense."

"*If* you believed in ghosts."

Beasley made his slow way toward us, slinking with his tummy almost to the ground. "See?" I asked Elizabeth. "Beasley has been freaked out since our ghostly friend walked into the store. Animals, they say, have a sense about these things. So what is up with that?"

Elizabeth knelt down to stroke Beasley's back. "Cats like their familiar places, and this one has been whisked off to somewhere new and strange." Then she walked around the store, picking up some honey-melon bath oil and a tin of mint tea. She presented them to me. "Home you go," she said, "for a soak and sip."

"Oh, that does sound tempting."

While books were our main business, I maintained a small display of wine glasses (exquisitely hand-painted), bath and body products, candles, and locally made chocolate. All things to enhance the experience of settling in with a good read—whether in a tub or comfy chair.

"Well, then, off I go." I stood and headed to the register to ring the items up. "You've talked me into it."

"Skip the register; go home," Elizabeth insisted. "The treats will be on me."

From my place at the counter, I stared down at the receipt the last customer had left. I'd been in too much of a state to put it properly away. The woman with the ghost's face had signed her name as "Elise Montgomery."

I took a mental note.

CHAPTER FOUR

*M*int tea and bath oil notwithstanding, I couldn't sleep that night. My mind was on Marguerite, who had been the very picture of cultured grace and pride—even in encounters with the surliest of guests. Fraud? Marguerite? No way. I'd seen her smile at a whining guest like he was her best friend. She might slip a to-go box of her oatmeal raisin cookies to a nightmare guest. "Emphasis on the *go*," she'd tell me later with a smile.

Now, as long as the chief pursued his current focus in the investigation, rumors would be flying about her business ethics. The only way to stop that was to solve the case myself, which was a little crazy. I *sold* books on murders; I'd *read* quite a few, but that hardly qualified me.

PENNY BROOKE

I did know an expert, though.

First thing after breakfast, I gave Andy a call. "Please tell me you have news," I said when he picked up at last.

"No arrest." He sighed. "But we did learn Marguerite had an altercation, a pretty heated one, with the crazy TV guy not long before she died. More than one of the other guests staying at the inn reported they had words."

A sense of relief surged through me; things seemed to be moving now toward a resolution. "And he had her brooch! How soon will it be before you lock him up?"

"Slow down! Not so fast. While his behavior is suspicious, he has an alibi. You see, we've narrowed down a window for the time she died—between eight a.m. and nine." He sighed. "Max Dakota in that hour was out in the back garden 'communing with the dead' like some kind of fool. They have it all on film."

"There was not a tiny bit of time in which he could have done it?" I sat down at the table with my second cup of coffee. "He was out there the whole hour?"

"The whole hour and beyond. Waking up a lot of guests who wanted to sleep in! Can you believe the nerve?" Andy let out a sigh. "Are there really people who believe the foolishness he spouts? You should have seen it, Rue, the way this guy swayed and moaned like a heart attack in progress. Then he claimed to have received a 'message' from a 'spirit' in the garden

46

—some type of romantic overture that was aimed at him!"

"Oh yeah, he has this idea he's some kind of Casanova." About once a month, like clockwork, some ghost of a young girl supposedly fell in love with him on the show. Which made me think their sight must have really started to go south once they reached the spirit world. Max then gently— and dramatically—proceeded to break their hearts—explaining that even the truest of true love cannot cross the boundaries of the mortal and spirit worlds.

"All for ratings, I suppose," said Andy.

"Yes, hearts will break in two after this word from our sponsors!" I let out a chuckle. "There's always something in the script to ramp up the drama. Like the ghost will reveal to Max where he hid the will or who put poison in his whiskey at the birthday dinner." I paused. "It could have been someone from his staff," I said. "Max could have told them what to do."

"Yeah, we thought of that. He's not off the hook. But most of them were out there in the garden with him, swaying in the perennials and roses, trampling the blooms." There was a level of disgust in Andy's voice.

"Marguerite loved her roses! She'd put in a new kind for Martinis in the Garden." Cared for them like the children she had never had.

"Our eyes are on the guy, but with the alibi and all, we don't have enough to make an arrest. Plus, there are other theories of how the thing went down."

"That stinks."

"Well, now, there are rules. We have to be sure, you know, and look at other possibilities as to the circumstances of her death."

"Like the fraud? That's nuts. You know that can't be right."

Andy paused. "There are many things you are not aware of, Rue. Let's just leave it at that."

I'd heard that tone before. It meant that very little—if any—information would be forthcoming on the topic.

"She was a good person," I insisted.

"Good people have their secrets too."

But her secrets were *good* secrets. *I may have good news soon...I think it will surprise you, and it's...well, it's rather nice.*

"Everyone has rights to their secrets, Andy."

He coughed. "Depends on the secrets, Rue. I know she was your friend, but things...weren't quite as they appeared."

What did he mean by that?

"Have you learned any more about that call she made about putting the inn up for sale?" I asked. "How serious was Marguerite about really taking off and leaving Somerset?"

"I am not at—"

"Liberty to say," I finished Andy's sentence for him. "All that talk of moving was probably some whim that had lasted for a second." I gazed out the window at the morning breeze. "We all dream of a different life some-times—when the tourists fill the town up in the summers and the days won't end."

Or maybe Marguerite *had* decided on a change. As closely as she was woven into the fabric of life in the Harbor, she had the right to go, to retire at sixty-seven if that was her choice. With more communities springing up to compete for tourists, the constant push to bring in business could have gotten to her.

Was that the "nice surprise" she had hinted at? A new life somewhere else?

Andy was quiet for a while, which meant I might get lucky. Sometimes he'd say more if I could wait him out. I took another sip of coffee.

"Something big was up," he said at last. "Lots of tears from Marguerite, who was normally so stoic."

"When was that?" I asked. "When she and Max Dakota had that fight?"

"On more than one occasion, she appeared to be

highly agitated in the weeks before her death. With Max and with others."

That tugged at my heart. "Oh, Andy, who said that?"

"That's based on the reports of several of our witnesses. And that combined with the sudden rush to get away…"

"Not necessarily a *rush*."

"Hey, the chief is waving at me, and I need to go."

"I won't keep you, Andy. Go and catch the bad guy."

A million questions fought for space in my head as I hung up and stared down at my phone. I had to somehow figure out why Marguerite had made that call to Beckham Properties.

I did know Brenda Shook, the manager and owner. I always let her know when new mysteries came in. And we used to walk together after work during my brief push to "build a fit and healthy Rue," inspired by a self-help title customers had raved about last spring.

I thought of Brenda as a friend, but I understood real estate professionals—much like my buddy Andy—were not "at liberty to say" everything they knew. I respected that.

At the same time, she might say *more*, would she not, to an "interested buyer?" Which I could pretend to be. Honesty's a virtue, but so is doing what one can to save the reputation of a friend.

Plus, I could stop by Captain Jack's and have a chat with Beth Arrington. She and Marguerite had a bond of sorts, although they were opposites in a lot of ways. Beth was loud and sometimes brash while Marguerite was soft and refined. But they often worked together to advocate our local charms and pull tourists into town. Two years ago the pair had launched a successful ad campaign that dangled the incentives of both the legendary hauntings at the Kingfisher Inn and the award-winning lobster rolls served at Captain Jack's. More recently, they had worked together to rally residents against the latest chain hotel, which, despite their efforts, had opened up last summer.

If Marguerite was feeling extra pressure to keep the inn in business, Beth might have been the one she confided in. Then the cops would have a way to explain the urge to sell the inn. Economics, after all, made much more sense than fraud!

I sent Elizabeth a text. "I was thinking I might take some more time off today—if that's okay with you."

I got back a thumbs-up. "Take whatever time you need," Elizabeth replied.

Now to make a plan.

CHAPTER FIVE

Martinis in the Garden. That could be my reason for checking in with Beth. She and her husband, Al, would be selling lobster rolls as well as the driftwood art Al created on the side. I had a packet to deliver with the location of the booths, vendor ID tags, and information sheets.

I threw on some blue capris and a casual white blouse, and soon I was pulling up at Captain Jack's. A beloved part of Somerset Harbor, the inn and restaurant were both housed in a gray sprawling building with a bright red roof. As soon as I opened my car door, I could smell the salty breeze and hear the rush of the ocean from behind the inn. The lot looked fairly empty, I was sad to note. It could just be an off week, or maybe this was normal with the tourists gone.

I made my way into the lobby with its plush blue chairs, the beach scenes in wood frames, and the captain's hats and nautical wooden wheels displayed throughout the room. Beth was behind the desk, checking a young family out. "We hope you'll come again," she told them with a smile, "and safe travels home." As the customers made their way out, the two youngest children racing toward the door, I approached the desk.

"Beth, how are you doing?"

"Hanging in, and you?"

"Still shaken up about Marguerite, if you want the honest truth, but I have the big event for distraction, which is good." I pulled a white folder from a canvas bag of festival paperwork. "I thought I would stop by with some vendor information for you. I can't believe it's in two weeks."

Beth had been an early skeptic of Martinis in the Garden with her worship of the way things "always had been done." As if the way to honor the rich history of the town was to keep the whole place stuck in the dusty days of yore—or 1970 at least. But she had come around when calls started coming in for rooms the weekend of the event. First, she heard from some young couples who fancied a martini (two martinis?) in the gardens and didn't want to drive the distance home to Provincetown or Chatham. Then calls had started coming in from nearby states as well.

"Thanks." She took the folder. "We're all in shock, I think. Just devastating news."

"The cops seem to be stumped." I leaned in and spoke quietly to Beth. "Did she ever talk to you about... someone who might have scared her, something on her mind? Anything at all?"

Beth smoothed down her neat ponytail, and I noticed a lot of brand-new silver had seeped into the brown. New lines seemed to have appeared in her face as well. One deepened in her forehead as she frowned. "I've tried to think about that, but she seemed fine to me," she said. "We tried to make a point of having coffee every Tuesday. She was my competitor, of course, but she was the only one who could understand the million aggravations of this line of work. I could complain to Marguerite, and Marguerite would get it." She looked around to make sure there were no guests about. "To be honest, Rue, customers in the last few years have simply gotten worse. Or maybe I'm just old."

"Was business good for Marguerite?"

Beth sighed. "Same as it is here. It could be a struggle, but she was making it. Of course, she had her ghost, which was her golden ticket. Even in poor weather, a well-publicized departed spirit is a major draw. From all over the US—and from *overseas*—people come to the Kingfisher to walk out in the gardens and listen for the ghost." A shadow crossed Beth's eyes. "Of course the poor captain and his pocket watch are all but forgotten now."

"The captain and his…?"

"Before the Kingfisher ghost, you see, people talked about *the captain*. Where do you think we get our name?" She pointed to a sign on the desk beside her. "Back in the day, the captain used to be *the* ghost—but of course you wouldn't know that as a newbie." She gave me a weary look, as if I had been the one to snatch the spotlight from her ghost. "He was included in some articles and ghost tours and the like, which was really nice. He brought in a little business, but what are you gonna do?" She shoved a brochure across the desk about Captain Jack's and pointed to a block of information on the back.

"Be Forewarned!" the caption said. "We've Been Told that Things Go Bump in the Night at Captain Jack's." The blurb told the story of the captain, who walked the shores at night looking for his family, who had all been drowned at sea. Guests were invited—if they dared—to walk along the beach and listen for the telltale signs of a ticking pocket watch.

"Interesting," I said.

"And then, just like that, there was a new ghost in town."

We were interrupted by the phone, which Beth promptly answered. "It's a great day at Captain Jack's. This is Beth. How may I help you?"

As she listened to the caller, her face went a little pale. "I understand. I do, but it's impossible right now." A hard look crossed her eyes. "But you know my situation. Surely you can...." She paused to listen for a moment. "I understand. I see." She hung up and closed her eyes, taking steady breaths.

"Is everything okay?" I asked.

"Of course." She put on a smile. "As we like to say, it's a great day at Captain Jacks! Despite what comes along, we have the salty breeze, food fresh from the sea!" She paused. "But running an inn—let me tell you, Rue—is not for the faint of heart."

"Which is why I wondered if Marguerite's...sudden end...was related to her business."

"I am really at a loss as to what might have happened. She didn't say a word about any recent trouble." Beth paused to think a moment. "Of course, I know at times she struggled—which is why I held my tongue on more than one occasion. I just let it go when she was written up for her Breakfast Delight, which anyone could see was the Hungry Captain's Sunrise

Special with a little dash of hot sauce and green onions."

In my head, I rolled my eyes. *Petty much? Good grief.* And what was up with that call?

"Always good to stick together," I replied.

"And we did just that. To be fair to Marguerite, she was very gracious when I borrowed one or two of her ideas as well. Like selling picnic baskets pre-packed for our guests to take out on the beach. She could have complained, I'm sure, but instead she gave me tips for keeping drinks and salads cold." Beth paused; her mind seeming somewhere else. She nodded toward the new-looking draperies with their nautical blue stripes. "Marguerite was kind enough to hook me up with a close friend of hers who let me have those curtains there for cost."

"How kind."

"Stupid online reviews. In the days before computers, customers could spread their vitriol to their friends and family but not to the whole world. 'Dingy, dated drapery' my foot! The old curtains were just fine, thank you very much. But after that, I braced myself for another bad review, which we could not afford." She straightened up a stack of brochures beside her. "Marguerite could see it was weighing on me, and she wasn't having that. We looked out for one another, she and I.

Both of us understood Somerset Harbor would lose a part of its character without the Kingfisher Inn or without Captain Jack's."

That was my opening to ask the very question I had come to ask. "So I guess she planned to stick around and run the Kingfisher for a while?"

"Well, I'd like to think *I myself* could be retired at sixty-seven. She was not a young woman, Marguerite. But retiring at that age is not a luxury all of us can afford. Plus, to Marguerite, the inn was home, and the people in the town were the only family she had." She sighed. "So she was here for life—a life that was cut too short."

Beth obviously didn't know her friend as well as she thought—and the same thing went for me.

Judith, Beth and Al's number two in charge, had wandered in while we were talking. She set her purse behind the counter.

"How was your time off?" asked Beth.

"Well, it was nice to be with family," Judith said, "but I was so disturbed by the news from home." The assistant manager was a heavy woman, having indulged in her fair share of the fish chowders, apple pies, and fried clams that were so plentiful in town. She heaved herself onto a stool beside the desk.

"Such a mystery," I said.

"Yeah, I saw her briefly the day before she died," said Judith. "I'd gone in with our deposit for the big event, and I got a real bad vibe coming off of her. She was not herself."

Beth looked at her, surprised. "You never mentioned that!"

"Well, you were out when I got back, and then I was out of town." Judith turned to me and smiled. "New grandbaby up in Boston."

"Oh, how nice," I said.

"A little girl. My daughter's first."

Beth waved to a guest heading out the door. "Sir, you enjoy your day!"

Then we both turned to Judith and almost spoke at once, asking about the last time she saw Marguerite.

"Well." Judith lowered her voice to a confiding tone. "She was sitting with a man when I walked into the lobby. The conversation looked...intense. And her eyes were red and puffy when she came up to take the check. Just a cold, she said. You know Marguerite. If it was personal, she would never talk about it; she did *not* let people in. But this guy, I could tell, had gotten her upset."

"So unlike Marguerite," said Beth. "She was unflappable."

"Was it Max Dakota? From the TV show?" I asked.

"Oh, no, it wasn't him. That guy would have stood out from a mile away."

This was getting complicated. I'd heard about a *young girl* who had upset Marguerite. Max was causing havoc, and now *another man* had been upsetting her as well? "What did he look like, this man?"

Judith raised an eyebrow. "Well, I am a married woman, but I still have eyes, and I have to tell you, Rue, this man was a looker."

"Oh, for goodness sake." Beth pursed her lips in disapproval. There was no room at all for fun in this woman's life; it had always been that way.

But I was more intrigued than I was amused. "A guest, a relative?" I asked.

"He might have been a guest because Marguerite insisted she could 'fix' whatever had disturbed him. That was the only thing I heard. He was an older man, in his seventies perhaps."

Beth's face had turned white as Judith told her story. Things seemed off with Beth as well.

I looked from Beth to Judith, whose description of the man had made me think of someone: the kind-eyed, distraught gentleman I'd met at the Kingfisher. "Joe Ripley," he had said when he'd introduced himself. "In town from New York." He had seemed so charming, so concerned. But wasn't that the way it always seemed to go with the true crime books that flew off the shelf? It never was some sleazy guy lurking around the corner. It was the best friend, the supposedly devoted husband, the grandmother from next door.

Was Joe still staying there? I'd have to check him out.

After a bit of small talk, I bid them goodbye. "Look the folder over, and just let me know if you have any questions. Each vendor gets one table, but we can find some extra space if needed. I know you'll have the lobster rolls and Al's driftwood sculptures too. Some of those, I know, can run pretty large." They tended toward artsy abstract shapes, all made from local driftwood. Tourists went crazy for the stuff, and Al Arrington turned them out pretty quickly. Well into his fifties, he was a ball of energy, always moving. If he wasn't combing local beaches for driftwood, he was carving his latest piece while he worked behind the desk at Captain Jack's.

"Oh, Al is slowing down," said Beth, to my surprise. "No extra space is needed. I guess we all are getting old."

That didn't seem to fit. I had seen him just last month, sprinting down the beach with a group of kids whose families, I assumed, were guests at Captain Jack's. The children all loved Al, and he would sometimes carve them tiny animals as free souvenirs.

"Well, I hate to hear that," I told Beth. "Both of you

take care. And, Beth, try to get some rest." I reached out to touch her hand. "We've all been through a lot."

Another canvas bag of folders still waited in my car, along with boxes of festival supplies that needed sorting through. I delivered some more folders since time was running short. I was on my own now as the sole orga- nizer—but my heart was no longer in the planning of the big event. Each cell in my body seemed to burn with the need to know who had murdered Marguerite.

My next stop: Beckham Properties, which would get me, hopefully, closer to an answer.

CHAPTER SIX

*T*he county's premier Realtors were housed in a low blue building one block to the left of the Seabreeze Bookshop. I made it a point to walk by— as if by chance—at a little bit past noon. At that time I knew Brenda would be likely to be pulling up with the top down on her BMW, hopping out and gathering her stuff from the car. During the off-season, Tuesday was her morning off unless there was a closing or out-of-towners were around to peep at a property.

The window featured posters of inviting-looking homes. A wooden sign above the door beckoned passersby: "How May We Help You Dream?"

Newer communities had sprung up over the past few years, giving Somerset Harbor competition for not only tourists but for buyers of second homes and beachfront properties. But Beckham, begun by Brenda's great-uncle, seemed to be prospering.

Right on cue, she drove up as I was studying the offerings in the window.

"Rue!" She got out of her car and smoothed down her long blonde hair, slightly tousled from the ride in the open air of a Massachusetts fall. "Hey, girl, I miss our walks. We should start back with that!" She put her hands on her hips. "Did you know a fudge shop is opening next door—next door to *me, a chocoholic?*" She rolled her eyes and laughed. "If I don't exercise, I'll expand like a balloon." She pulled a large Gucci bag out of her car and threw it across her shoulder.

"I could use the exercise, believe me." I reached toward her bag and stuffed in some flyers that threatened to spill out. "This morning I decided I just had to stretch my legs. For stress relief, you know. What with Martinis in the Garden and now—"

"Marguerite!" Her eyes grew wide. "Oh Rue, it's unbelievable."

"I got so much closer to her in the past few weeks—because of the event, you know. She was such a presence in this town. That laugh, that energy!" I looked down at the ground. "It just seems impossible that she isn't here."

"Yeah, I sent all my out-of-towners there to get a room, and she was never less than gracious. Every client that I sent there raved about the place—and they all loved Marguerite."

Time to execute the plan.

"She was a master hostess," I agreed. "That much is for sure, and I know the job was harder than it looked. I was hoping when the festival was over, she could have a little sit-down with my cousin Erin. That is Erin's dream now—to open up an inn, and I thought Marguerite could give her a true picture of the day-to-day, the good and the bad."

"That would have been so perfect."

"What I wouldn't give for Erin to move here to Somerset," I said. "But what this town *doesn't* need is another inn." I paused. "Of course, now that…I imagine that the heirs will keep the Kingfisher as it is. Heather, I suppose, will stay on and run it. She's been with Marguerite for years."

"Well, you know…" Brenda paused, seemingly unsure whether to go on.

"Erin and I used to joke as kids we'd open businesses in the same town when we grew up. And meet for lunch every day!" I smiled ruefully. "It would have been kind of cool to really make that happen, but what can you do? I think she's found an inn for sale—one she really likes— and I say good for her. Too bad it's in Vermont." I shrugged.

There was a long pause.

"Has she signed a contract yet?"

"Getting close, I think."

Again, Brenda hesitated.

Could this crazy plan be working? Was she about to spill?

"Do you have time to come in for a coffee?" Brenda asked. "You won't believe this headache, and every fiber of my being is screaming for caffeine."

"Oh, how nice. I'd love to. We do need to catch up."

She unlocked the door and led me into the small, well-appointed office decorated in ocean greens and blues. She dropped her stuff, turned on the lights, got the coffee going, and soon we were settled in, her behind her desk and me across from her on a leather love seat.

Brenda took a breath. "Okay, here's the deal. I can't say too much right now, but since you are a friend, I will just tell you this. You might want to tell your cousin to hold off a little longer—that is if she can. I plan very soon to announce a property that might be perfect for her—very close to you."

I looked up at her, pretending to be surprised. In fact, I *was* surprised. I had understood from Andy that Marguerite had put out some feelers on a price and the amount of time it might take for the inn to sell. But now it almost seemed that Marguerite had firmed up a deal with Brenda.

I sat back and pretended to mull over what she'd said. "Well, the competition here is tough," I mused. "With those dreadful chains and all—no personality at all. Just zero." I rolled my eyes at Brenda. "They had really cut into Marguerite's ability to keep the inn filled up. And with the Kingfisher so established, and also Captain Jack's, I just don't want to set my cousin up to fail—if you know what I mean."

"Well, if she would like to buy an inn with a solid reputation—and only *one* competitor with any local flair —she might be in luck." Her look signaled there was more she couldn't say. "Then you two could be in town together, doing business in the Harbor." She took a sip of coffee. "I wish I had family here. None of my aunts or uncles got around to having children, so it's dwindled to just me. Where is your cousin from?"

"She's been in Concord for two years. I do admit I'd love to see Erin living here." I cocked my head to study Brenda. "So, really, what's the deal? Is Captain Jack's for sale? Because Erin found this great place in Grafton…"

Brenda hesitated. Then she shook her head. "No, not Captain Jack's."

"Not the Kingfisher surely. With all the press it gets, I

imagine that the heirs—whoever they might be—would hold on to the place."

My friend leaned in and spoke quietly. "I was already under contract to put it up for sale before…well, you know. Marguerite came to me about it not long before she died. She asked me to hold off on the advertisement till she could tell the people she was closest to in town."

Bingo. I was getting somewhere now. "She was selling? Why?"

"You know, it was kind of weird. I asked where she was going, and she did everything she could to get me off the subject. It was very clear she didn't want to say." Brenda shrugged. "None of my business really, but it struck me as odd because Marguerite and the Kingfisher Inn—they've been institutions here forever."

"Was there something wrong, you think?"

"Not really. I don't think so. She had a kind of… spark. And I remember thinking that I wanted to be just like Marguerite when I hit my sixties. Off on some adventure that would shock this little town! Because that was the vibe I got, that Marguerite was doing something *for herself*." Brenda sighed. "And then when I heard what happened, I thought about how happy she had been that day she came in to sign. Oh Rue, what could have happened to her? Who in the world—and why?" She paused, lost in thought. "She said she was finally going off to live the life she was always meant for." Brenda picked up her coffee mug. "Seemed to me she was right there in her element already, hosting guests and putting out those enormous spreads." She stared down into her mug. "I guess you never know what a person really wants."

The life she was always meant for—what could that even mean?

"So, what happens now?" I asked.

"Still figuring that out. We are working with the lawyers and the heirs, and we'll see how it goes."

"Who are the heirs exactly? She never spoke of family."

"Oh, I've already run my mouth way more than I should have. I just felt the listing seemed too perfect for your cousin. So, there's my little hint that this might be worth a wait. Just between you and me, of course, and maybe Erin too, if this holds an interest for her."

"Oh, sure. I understand, and I appreciate the tip."

Brenda rubbed at her forehead, frowning, and I noticed for the first time she was not herself. Most days her energy was a fifteen out of ten; today it seemed stuck at five or six. In her eyes I saw a weariness that had never been there.

"Hey, Brenda, you okay?"

"Yeah." She let out a sigh. "Everything is fine. It's just

that this whole business with the inn has been super weird." She screwed up her forehead. "Like, some really crazy stuff started going on as soon as I got the listing. And then *somebody goes and strangles Marguerite.*"

Were those tears in Brenda's eyes?

She lowered her voice to a whisper. "Rue, I'm really scared."

I leaned forward in my chair. "Oh, Brenda! What is going on?"

"Well, when the letters started, they were polite, you know?"

"Letters?"

"They started almost right away once we had signed the contract. 'We ask respectfully that the inn be sold as a private home to cut back on competition for beloved locals. Please do so in the spirit of neighbors helping neighbors.' They were, of course, unsigned."

"Any clue who could have sent them?"

"Rue, I have no idea. Lots of people, I suppose, could have been her competition. The hotels, the bed and breakfasts, the caterers in town."

Since the recent downturn, Marguerite had expanded into catering and had also opened up the inn for weddings—which had not been well received by the owners of event halls and historic homes. This was an old town, whose residents—and their families before them—held on possessively to their long-held niches. I'd pitied the poor man who just the year before set up a muffin case in the back of Mayflower Deli. The locals had rallied around our already established "muffin man" as if war had been declared. The Mayflower Deli promptly switched to sweet potato pies.

Brenda rubbed at her left temple. "And the thing about it was, no one was supposed to even know the inn was up for sale. How did they find out?" She paused. "Then it got even worse. My tires were cut last week, and then right after that, someone slipped a note beneath the door."

"What did it say?" I asked, appalled.

"It said they were hoping I'd do the right thing. I had quietly reached out to a potential buyer who would keep the property as is; they would run it as an inn. But that didn't pan out, and I guess the word got out. But *how* did it get out? Someone is watching me. And that freaks me out in a major way."

"That is just horrific."

"Of course I called the cops. And of course their main advice was not to say a word. You know how it is. We must uphold the image splashed across the ads. *Discover, Dream, and Play with Us. Somerset Harbor: Your Carefree Corner in the Sun.* Any crimes are supposed to be our little secret."

"Did they give you *real* advice, like how to protect yourself?" I was fuming now. "I hope they're investigating."

She shrugged. "They checked the note for fingerprints. They asked a lot of questions. We'll see how it goes." She rubbed above her temple. "And now that I am thinking the threats might be connected to a murder? Well, sometimes I can't breathe."

"Be very careful, Brenda."

She gave me a small smile. "I might have blown a sale by telling you all this. But if they make an arrest real soon—for the murder, for the vandalism—it could be an awesome deal for your cousin, a gorgeous property."

"Oh, Erin's always been the tough one. Nothing bothers Erin." Which was a big advantage of being nonexistent.

We traded a few theories about who could be behind the notes. Then when a customer came in, I slipped out quietly with a little wave. "We'll keep in touch," I said.

I headed to the little park in the middle of the square just to sit and think. My mind was almost bursting with the complications of the case. We had a half-mad TV kook who communed with the dead, and we had the ghostly lookalike of some tragic figure from Somerset Harbor's past. We had Marguerite's desire to run off to fulfill some long-harbored dream. And then there was the kindly seeming Joe, who had caused Marguerite to weep.

And now we could add to that an angry letter writer who somehow had discovered the inn was up for sale—and was adamant about its future use. Impassioned enough about it to slash Brenda's tires—and to murder Marguerite?

To get my mind off the murder, I pulled out my phone and saw my screen was filled with texts. All of them concerned Martinis in the Garden.

"Need space near the front," said one.

"What time can we set up?" asked another.

"Alpacas double booked and unavailable as scheduled. Refund of your deposit is forthcoming. Please see the attached."

Banquo's ghost and Macbeth's Witches! We needed those alpacas. Students even now were immersed in alpaca units. Essays had been written! In store windows across town, stuffed alpacas frolicked with the latest merchandise. The idea of an appearance by alpacas had generated more excitement than I would have ever guessed.

I closed my eyes and sighed. I knew headaches weren't contagious, but I seemed to have caught the one Brenda couldn't shake.

CHAPTER SEVEN

*E*lizabeth finally picked up.

"Alpaca emergency!" I said, inching away from the very affectionate creature nuzzling my arm. The alpaca's tongue was tickly as I reached out to pet its nose. "Good girl, Buttercup," I said, keeping my voice gentle.

A second one, Bartholomew, moved into the action. And now here came a third!

"Apparently," I whispered to Elizabeth, "I'm the alpaca whisperer. No interest from a man in six months at least, but the alpacas are big fans."

"Why are you *with alpacas*?" she asked after a pause. "If you're uncomfortable around them, Rue, simply step away. But I do hear they are gentle—very friendly."

"Very, very friendly." One of them licked my elbow,

gazing at me with big eyes. Then things seemed to calm down as two of the alpacas strolled over to some children. I stroked the other's neck. "Things are good," I told Elizabeth. "It's fine."

She let out a gentle laugh. "Hardly an emergency. Where are you anyway? Did you decide alpacas are the new cure for stress? I approve! I love it."

"The emergency is that the alpacas bailed from Martinis in the Garden—and I need new ones fast." I explained the situation. I apologized profusely since I'd had to drive quite a distance on my tour of alpaca farms.

"I've got this, Rue," she said. "I can keep things going at the store. You do what you have to. I know your plate is full."

"You are the best," I said. Maybe when all of this was over, we could have a spa day; both of us deserved it.

It had been a day. On my way out of town, I'd gone back to Captain Jack's to retrieve my bag—which I'd left on the counter earlier that day. Too much was on my mind, and I was getting sloppy. Inside were vendor folders and essential paperwork for the big event. *Sheesh. Get it together, Rue.*

Inside Captain Jack's, things had seemed very quiet, and I had felt unsettled by the stillness of the place. I'd always thought of Captain Jack's as the louder, more rambunctious of our two local inns. It drew the young families with children while the Kingfisher was for elegant romantic getaways or mother-daughter trips.

This afternoon, you could have heard a pin drop, which was quite a contrast to the Captain Jack's I knew.

"Hello!" I called out at the front desk, but no answer came. I knocked on the door beside the desk with the sign marked "Office."

"Beth, are you there? It's Rue."

When I got no answer, I opened the door and peeked in. No Beth, Al, or Judith, but there was my bag. *Thank Anna Karenina and Jane Eyre!* I slipped in to grab it, and that's when I saw the envelope on top of a stack of mail. The red stamped letters seemed to shout at me: "Fore-closure, Second Notice."

For the second time that week, my heart broke in two.

I grabbed my bag and hurried through the lobby and then out the door, unsettled. I was lost in thought when Beth appeared from around the corner.

"Rue!" She looked surprised. "I was just cleaning up in back."

I held up the bag. "I left this like a fool, but now all is good."

"Oh, well, I'm glad to hear it. I guess you saw Judith and she got you squared away."

Not really but I nodded.

She gave a little wave, and I was on my way.

I leaned against the wall and closed my eyes, still shaken. What a disturbing week. I dropped the bag in my car and caught a strong whiff of the sea air, which calmed me down a little, along with the scent of jasmine growing on the property.

I glanced down at my cell for the time. I had time for just a quick peek at the waves; it would do me good. New Englanders soon learn just a brief glance at the water is a cheap but effective balm.

As I walked back toward the inn, a familiar figure came around the same corner Brenda had.

"Joe!" I said, surprised.

The older man looked at me, startled. Then he composed himself and smiled.

I held out my hand. "Rue. I'm a friend of Marguerite's. I met you yesterday at the Kingfisher Inn."

"Oh, Rue! Yes, of course. I was just out for a quick stroll. Such a lovely town you have!" He jammed his hands deep into the pocket of his khaki pants and stared down at the ground. "But now, I'm afraid, I really have to run. Big appointment, don't you know. Always late, it seems!" He nodded to me politely. "But very good to see you, Rue."

I watched him walk away, confused. It really made no sense for Joe to be walking here. Right outside his room at the Kingfisher were lots of garden paths and easy water access. No need to come this far for "a quick stroll."

I had to clear my head, so maybe it was good I had a reason for a nice long drive to commune with alpacas. After a brief peek at the sea, I walked back to my car. I set my list of alpaca farms on the seat beside me and queued up my playlist.

CHAPTER EIGHT

*S*oon I had secured the services of Bartholomew and Buttercup, who came at quite a price, putting me way over budget for Martinis in the Garden. I suspected that their owner, the beady-eyed and watchful Eddie James, could smell the desperation coming off of me. While his fleecy charges were affectionate and gentle, Eddie was the opposite: loud-mouthed and determined to squeeze every penny he could get out me: a feeding fee, transportation add-on charges, fees for the handlers… The list went on and on.

Buttercup looked on as I put my signature on the dotted line. Sympathy seemed to well up in her big eyes, as if she were apologizing for the behavior of her owner.

With the festival back on track, I began the long drive home, knowing Marguerite would have waved away my worries over the unexpected costs. "You did it for the children," she would have reassured me. "We'll find the money, Rue."

Her voice in my head sounded very sure—but she didn't tell me *where* to look for these elusive funds.

I could also hear Bill Bright's gravelly scolding now. "Expensive frippery!" he'd say if I couldn't somehow manage to make the numbers work.

Hmm. It had been easy enough, I supposed, for *him* to stay on budget when his tired event was just the same old drudgery he put on every year. Somerset Harbor deserved better than dull and mediocre!

As often was the case, one of my beloved writers popped into my head to give better voice to my rambling thoughts.

Mediocrity knows nothing higher than itself. That was Arthur Conan Doyle, whose books I really should pull off the shelves and delve into again. I loved a juicy crime *when it stayed on the pages* and out of my real life. Plus, I needed the distraction of an absorbing read. Sherlock, take me away!

I pulled onto the main road, cataloging in my head the expenses that remained for the big event. I'd have to make some cuts.

Flyers! Those could go, of course. Who needed *flyers* in a town of world-class gossips? If there was a new flavor at Sweet Dreams Bakery or if someone sprained an ankle on their way into work, everybody knew by the time the early lunch line formed at Crabby Cathy's.

I knew I had done what I'd had to do. The alpacas were the thing to bring the town together at our fall event. The teetotalers, of course, could refuse a nice martini. The dull and the straitlaced could turn their noses up at the gardens and the art. But even Bill's mouth had tugged up into something like a smile when I had brought out the photos of alpacas during our initial pitch.

I drove on for a while, glad to have, at least, a change in scenery. But in the silence of the car, my mind went back to the murder. The urgent need to save my friend's reputation hit me once again like a boulder to my chest. If I didn't find some answers, Bob Lee would latch on even harder to the ugly rumors in his rush to solve the case. Any talk of fraud on the part of Marguerite had to be a lie.

Stopping for a light, I eyed my cellphone sitting snugly in its holder on the dashboard. I was way overdue for a long chat with Andy. I had to tell him that Joe Ripley was acting really odd. That guy for sure should be on officials' radar. I wondered if Andy was aware how much trouble Beth was in with money—and how much her resentment of Marguerite still simmered.

Plus, there was something that stuck out from my talk with Brenda. Marguerite's future plans had been a happy, joyful thing. Brenda had seemed sure! There had been no sense of shame or need of escape—just something new for Marguerite, some delicious secret.

If she had sold a little earlier, left sooner than she planned, she would still be alive. Tears prickled in my eyes. Even the glories of a Massachusetts fall outside my window couldn't ease the knot deep inside my chest. On my left was the surprise of a cranberry bog spread out in all its vibrant glory, but the beauty of the sight was wasted on the likes of me. The verdant green just up ahead held no comfort for me, nor did the canopy of reds and yellows tunneling over traffic.

At the next stoplight, I punched on Andy's name and put the phone on speaker.

He answered after two rings. "Things are crazy, Rue. I can give you half a second."

A pretty useless block of time. I noticed an odd humming sound in the background on his end. "Where the heck are you?"

"I'm back at the Kingfisher—where Max Dakota, as per usual, is refusing to behave."

"Is that chanting that I hear?"

"Supposedly, there are spirits in the lobby—a whole darn party's worth. The chanting is his way of trying to encourage them to communicate with him." Andy let out a sigh. "Heather has asked him nicely to take all his nonsense to a more private place. He's kind of freaking out the guests. But he hasn't budged."

"Oh, what a mess for Heather. I can just imagine."

"Now he's screeching something about spirits—more spirits than he's ever seen—trying to break through with urgent messages." A note of amusement crept into Andy's voice. "Apparently we have Dwight D. Eisenhower right here in the lobby! Marilyn Monroe! The camera guys are going nuts."

"Quite a party I would say. I hope you dressed for the occasion."

"This whole display just reeks of disrespect. Rue, this is insane." Andy spat out the words. "This charlatan Max Dakota surely has the footage that he needs for his thirty-minute show. He should take his toys and go. People here are mourning, and poor Heather, I'm afraid, is hanging by a thread."

"Why don't you make him leave?"

"That will happen soon."

I slowed as traffic started building up. "Well, since I've used up that half second that you promised, I will save *my* news. Any news from your end besides the party of A-listers who've descended on our town?"

"Yes, in fact, there is." Andy lowered his voice. "We've

made a list of missing jewelry, and it's quite extensive, Rue. So theft is looking like the likely motive for the murder."

Theft, not fraud. *Of course.*

He let out a sigh. "The lady didn't skimp when it came to pretty baubles. There were diamonds; there were rubies, all of a *significant* quality and size. Earrings, bracelets, the works."

Marguerite had always loved the finer things, and she wore them with style.

"Well, at least Bob understands that she didn't die because she did something wrong," I said. "No more victim blaming!"

"Not so fast," said Andy. "No one's shaming Marguerite; she did not deserve to die. But the question of some kind of fraud is not off the table yet. The thing we don't know is if our perpetrator was acting out of simple greed—or to collect on something someone thought they were owed."

"She didn't owe a thing," I huffed.

"Heather made a list of some of the more pricey pieces she had seen her wear. And when we checked her room and the business safe, most of the more expensive baubles were nowhere to be found."

Traffic picked up a little, and I put my foot on the

gas, inching forward just a bit. "That looks bad for our ghost hunter. We know he had her brooch."

"Lots of marks against him. Look, Rue, I need to run. That nutso Max Dakota is *standing* on the desk—and with a whole line of guests who are trying to check out."

I could hear Max shouting. "Some of the spirits of this place long to check out too! And move on to their eternal rest. But first I must convince them to release their burdens to me." That was followed by a high-pitched sound—something in between singing and a wail. I could hear murmurs in the background.

"Now the guy is turning with his hands up in the air," said Andy. "Talk to you later, Rue!"

Well, sheesh.

Traffic slowed again, and I mulled over Andy's news about the thefts. His descriptions of the jewelry had stirred up something in my mind that now came into focus: Elise Montgomery in the store! She had bought two books on antique treasures and heirlooms. And now Marguerite's antique treasures had been snatched away.

I turned on a little music to try to give my mind some rest. As I passed more fall scenery, I said a silent prayer of thanks for Elizabeth, who'd worked most of the day without me. But the store, at least, should be fairly quiet with the tourists gone. And she'd have time to work on her Families Through the Years exhibit, which would make her happy. Elizabeth was never happier than when she was staring into some old photo, transported to another time. She had once confided that she wished she'd lived back in the fifties. "I just love the clothes, the civility, the quieter way of life," she'd said.

"But think how old you'd be!" I had told her. "Eighties babies rule."

"You have a point." She'd held up a photo. "But would you look at this hat? At no time in this century could I get away with this fabulous creation."

"I'd rather keep my cell phone, my dishwasher, all the gifts that ease the life of modern hatless woman," I'd replied.

Now I smiled at the memory. It was a debate the two of us had enjoyed for years.

My thoughts were diverted by a small hand-lettered sign advertising lobster chowder just ahead. A bowl of chowder, bread, and salad was the Thursday special at a place called Libby's Kitchen, just three miles away. It was almost time for dinner, and I'd had no time for lunch. Now my mouth was watering at the thought of chowder.

As directed by the sign, I turned off the main road onto a two-lane street, my spirits already lifting at the thought of food. But soon I fell behind a gray Nissan that was traveling at an infuriating fifteen miles an hour. A loud rattling coming from the car was a big hint why.

I could partly sympathize. Car trouble absolutely stunk. All of us had been there. But could the driver not pull over and let a person pass?

Then almost instantly, my irritation turned to guilt. Okay, I was hungry, but this poor person in the Nissan had much bigger problems than a growling stomach.

Slowing to a crawl, I stared at the triangular scuff mark on the Nissan's bumper. It kind of looked familiar, along with the sticker advertising the Somerset Harbor Woman's Club. Hmm. *Someone else from home* was out this far as well. We must be more than twenty miles from the Somerset Harbor city limits. Quite a coincidence, I mused.

Perhaps they could use a lift back home. After some lunch, of course—if Libby's Kitchen didn't close before I could creep the slow miles left to the restaurant. I could taste that chowder now.

Andy, of course, would warn me away. That old "stranger-danger" thing they used to teach in school. I could hear him now. "Your good intentions, Rue, will one day come back to bite you."

Well, what would he have me do? Leave some member of the woman's club to rattle her way home with a car that might *explode* or stop dead in the road?

The Andy in my head was just being an alarmist! As if murderers, kidnappers, and the like could possibly be members of the Somerset Harbor Woman's Club.

Finally deciding to give up, the driver pulled over to the side and brought the Nissan to a stop. Part of me wanted to speed up toward that chowder and that thick piece of buttered bread, but the better Rue pulled over.

Then the car door opened and, much to my amazement, out stepped...Beth.

What was she doing here?

I jumped out of my car. "Quite a coincidence," I said. "What are you doing out this way?"

I watched her face turn white when she recognized my voice. Then she wheeled around to look at me, alarmed. Not the reaction I expected. "I...just had some errands," she began, "and this old car picked the perfect time to...well, I have no idea what the heck is up with the car."

"Can I take you anywhere? We could look up an auto shop."

"Oh! I can just call Al." She sighed. "We'll have to figure out if there's a way to fix this that won't break the bank." She looked like she might dissolve into sobs right there on the spot.

"I was heading down the road. To get some lobster chowder! Why don't you come with me? I can buy you a nice meal while you wait for Al. It's better, don't you think, than waiting in the car? It will take Al a while to get here all the way from Somerset."

She looked warily at her car. "Oh, I couldn't leave the Nissan. Al will be along."

"Oh, I think you deserve a treat." I gave her a sympathetic smile. "And it's almost as if fate sent me to find you here in the middle of nowhere."

"Well…I really can't, but thanks." She looked nervously again at her car. There seemed to be something there she didn't want to leave. Marguerite's rings and necklaces perhaps? Was there too big a haul to cram into the small black purse I could see inside?

Instantly, I was embarrassed by the thought. This, after all, was *Beth,* who was prickly for sure but was a stalwart of our town. This was Beth, who was mourning Marguerite, possibly a dying business, and now a misbehaving car.

Today she seemed oddly formal. "Rue, I do appreciate it, but I'd prefer to wait right here."

"Okay…if you're sure?"

"I am."

"Well, you have my cell. If you need me, Beth, just call."

CHAPTER NINE

*A*fter a satisfying dinner, I checked for any messages or texts that might have come from Beth. Instead, I found a text from Andy.

He was replying to a question I had sent him earlier while waiting for my food. Gazing out the window, I had noticed an advertisement for a pawnshop down the road. So I had idly texted Andy, hoping for a little "company" while they prepared my meal.

"Checking pawnshops, I presume," I had texted him.

When he hadn't answered right away, I'd shoved my phone into my purse and pulled out a paperback. Bookstore owners come prepared!

Now, I read his response. "We have feelers out at all the local ones. No matches, but it's early."

I got back on the road, hoping the traffic hadn't gotten worse. I was anxious now to get back to the store, but I'd check in first with Beth. My meal had come out quickly, so there was a good chance Al had not arrived.

But someone else, it seemed, had now stopped to help. A silver Mercedes was parked behind the Nissan. That car definitely wasn't Al's.

I slowed to take a look. Beth seemed to be scrambling to gather items from her car. A man stood nearby watching with his back to me.

Then she straightened up, a small silk bag in her hand just as she caught sight of me. As it had before, her face turned white. She said something to the man, who turned.

Whoa. I knew that man. Joe's face looked alarmed before he lifted his hand—very hesitantly—in a tiny wave.

Heavens to Harry Potter. Alarm bells were clanging in my head. Joe and Beth together? And a pawnshop down the road—not as well-known, I was sure, to our local cops as our local pawnshops.

With no other traffic on the road, I came to a stop and rolled my window down. I forced myself to smile. "Everything okay here? Need anything from me?"

Beth's voice came out like a squeak, unlike her usual

robust way of speaking. "Thank you, Rue. We're good. Joe has come to help."

How did she know *Joe*? What was the connection? I had to talk to Andy—and ASAP. At the first convenient spot, I pulled into a parking spot and sent him a text. "Pawnshop. Kennedy Chase Drive. Outside of Barnstable. Trust me—check it out." At the last minute, I typed in, "Drinks tonight after work?"

I was not above breaking out my stash of good liquor to loosen Andy's tongue. We were due for one of our somewhat regular "porch talks." Both of us loved the wide front porch of the home that used to be my gran's. When she retired, I'd moved into her house and taken over the bookstore that she had owned for years. Along with keeping readers entertained, I'd upheld another of her beloved traditions: serving Andy cocktails and solving all the problems of the world with him as we enjoyed the salty breeze.

After fighting a knot of traffic closer into town, I pulled in at last to the Seabreeze Bookshop. I found Elizabeth intent on her work, photos spread around her on her table in the corner.

"Welcome back," she called as Gatsby yipped out his own greeting. Beasley peeked out curiously from behind the biographies, and Oliver meowed as he sprang out from the cookbook section. I recognized that meow. It meant "Feed me now."

"Sorry!" I called out, pulling off my coat. "What a busy day." I would save the news about Joe and Beth for Andy. I couldn't figure out what to think about it, and my head would ache if I gave it much more thought. I reached for the pet treats in the bottom drawer next to the register.

Elizabeth looked up, a serious look in the set of her mouth. "I have news—about your ghost."

I startled, almost spilling the bag of treats onto the floor. "You have news? About Elise?"

"No, not the customer—who is the *modern* version of the ghost. I've found out some things about the fifties version."

As I approached her table, Elizabeth held out another picture of the woman from the picnic. This time, the four little girls were piled into her lap, laughing at the camera, all in matching sleeveless dresses. "Look closely," said Elizabeth. "Tell me what you see."

"Well, from the dates on the other photo, I am seeing precious children who don't have long to live—or *three* of them don't." The smallest one, in the foreground, gave me a shy smile, like she knew a secret. I wished there were a way to jump into the photo and save her from…whatever.

"They were swept away to sea by a giant wave back in fifty-four," Elizabeth explained, standing up to look over my shoulder. She let out a sigh. "One of our bigger storms. I can barely think about it. I found an article in one of the old newspapers that I keep in back. But you're missing something, Rue. Look closely at the photo." She let out a breath. "Besides a mother and her daughters, what is it you see?"

That's when I recognized the elaborate points of the roofline and the scattered balconies. I gasped. "They're at the Kingfisher! They're at Marguerite's."

"Back then it wasn't hers," said Elizabeth. "In those days, it was a private home. Back then the house belonged to Thomas and Sarah Perkins—or, as you might refer to her, the *ghost*."

So *this* version of the ghost went by the name of Sarah—and she had owned the Kingfisher property before it was Marguerite's. Now, she kept watch in a place of honor on the top row of photos in the lobby of the inn.

"Sarah herself died more than forty years ago," said Elizabeth. She picked up a yellowed newspaper page that appeared to be mostly obituaries.

I thought of my favorite ghost stories, which had first captivated me when I was a young girl spellbound by a campfire. These days I gravitated toward more literary ghosts who wandered by the sea or down the lonely corridors of decrepit castles.

Elizabeth looked sadly at the photo. "If she got to choose, don't you think she'd come at the age she is right here? When she was at her happiest, when she had all her girls."

"That's what I *would* believe. If I believed in ghosts." I paused. "Sarah Perkins. What do you know about her?" Elizabeth seemed to have been busy in my absence.

She handed me the obit. "She was a longtime widow. Had one daughter who survived. The daughter's name was Henrietta, but she seemed to go by 'Hetty.'"

"The daughter who we think was friends with Marguerite back when they were young."

"I've found other pictures too." Elizabeth lined them up on the table. "Marguerite and Hetty seemed to have been quite close. At one time they were, at least. Then there is no trace of Hetty after the seventies or so."

One picture showed them at the beach. In another photo, they were standing by a car, suitcases in their hands, waving to the camera. In several other photos, they were making funny faces or smiling arm in arm. There was no mistaking Marguerite, who even in her twenties had the same elegant, warm smile. Her dark hair was slightly wavy and looked soft to the touch. Hetty was shorter with a thick curtain of light hair that fell around her shoulders; her smile was more reserved than her effervescent friend's.

"And here they are with Sarah, Hetty's mom." Elizabeth handed me a photo of the girls sitting beside an older version of the ghost. With a few less wrinkles and a cloche-style hat perched jauntily atop her curls, she would be the woman in the portrait at the Kingfisher Inn.

Marguerite had always hinted she had no idea who the woman in the portrait was, but Marguerite, as I was learning, was a woman who had secrets.

Overwhelmed with all the news of the day, I sunk into one of the chairs Elizabeth kept around the table. "So, we have no idea what became of Hetty?"

"No clue, unfortunately. After Sarah died, Hetty seems to have disappeared from any of the pictures of the goings-on in town." Elizabeth had amassed extensive photograph collections—some from professionals who had been paid by families or groups or the now-defunct *Somerset Harbor Bee*.

Oliver was weaving anxiously around my feet. He had seen the treat bag, and he was insistent it was time to get his snack. But my mind was spinning; my mind veered to Elise. "That customer—the woman, Elise Montgomery," I mused. "Do you think she might be in town to visit family here? Her resemblance to this Hetty is uncanny."

"I had the exact same thought. It almost seems the two of them would have to be related."

I ran my hand through my hair. "So, let's think for a minute about everything we know. Elise is at the inn the week Marguerite is killed. Then she comes into our store to get some books on *heirlooms*." I took a breath. "Andy said to me today that most of Marguerite's expensive jewelry has gone missing."

Elizabeth stared at me, her eyes growing wide. "And now it seems the family who used to own the inn might be related to Elise."

I thought of Andy's words in the aftermath of the discovery of the body. *Let's just say for now a fight was overheard, and there were accusations. The person spoke of "theft" and "abuse of trust."* Was he referring to a conversation between Elise and Marguerite?

Joe had seen Marguerite and a "young lady" having words. He had told me that in our first conversation. The gorgeous property the inn was situated on must be worth a pretty penny. Had Marguerite come to own it in a not-so-legal way?

I waved the thought away. That was ridiculous.

Oliver mewed plaintively at me, a question in his cries. You would never know he'd had two full meals

PENNY BROOKE

that day. Beasley and Gatsby, too, were watching me
eagerly. Beasley was standing very still while Gatsby
panted happily. Six huge eyes in total were intent on me.

As I handed out the goodies, I wondered if there
were other family members still in town connected to
Sarah, Hetty, and the others in the Perkins clan.

As she often did when it came to all things vintage
Somerset Harbor, Elizabeth answered the question in
my head before I could even speak it. "No other family's
mentioned in the obituary. According to some other
things I've found, Marguerite seems to have opened the
inn a year or so after Sarah died."

"Interesting," I said. "She might have spent some time
there when she was friends with Hetty." There would be
records, of course, of any sale. I'd add that to my list of
questions to ask Andy—if I could ever catch him long
enough to really talk.

The Bookstore Three brushed up against my legs for
a second round of treats, tickling my shins. "These guys
love their food," I said, digging back into the bag.

Elizabeth neatened a stack of pictures. "I have to
assume Hetty moved away and may be living somewhere under a married name."

I held out my hands with the treats, and three warm
tongues descended on them. "Or she could have stayed
in town," I said. "I'm sure a ton of people don't show up

in your pics. It could have been that Hetty developed camera shyness." I raised an eyebrow at my friend. "That can happen to a woman—after a certain age that will not be named."

"Oh, yeah, don't I know it," said Elizabeth with a grin. "As much as I love to curate other people's photos, I don't want any cameras pointed at *this* face." She shuffled through more photos. "Oh, don't get me wrong. I have earned my wrinkles; I've embraced them. But I will leave the posing to the younger girls."

"So perhaps she stuck around," I said. Could Hetty still live here in town?

"Oh, I don't think she stayed, Rue, or she would have attended this—the grand opening of the Kingfisher Inn." Elizabeth presented me with a photo of a young Marguerite at the ribbon cutting, surrounded by a large group of smiling people, including town officials. With a rush of amusement, I picked out a young Bill Bright.

Elizabeth continued, "This would have been, you'd think, a big day for Hetty too. It was the house where she grew up. And it was a big step for Marguerite, who seemingly was one of Hetty's closest friends."

"I adore this photo." I studied it more closely. "Marguerite would have loved to have this for her wall. But I suppose you're right. I'd think Hetty would have been there if she was still in town."

"She's blessed and well, I hope." Elizabeth closed her eyes as if in silent prayer. It seemed to trouble her sometimes not to be assured of happy endings for the people in her photos. She saw a lot of starts and middles when it came to other people's stories, told through her vintage photos. But she rarely saw the endings. She witnessed only moments, tiny bits of captured life.

Now, her eyes were twinkling. "I saved the big news for last," she told me with a wink.

I sat up at attention.

"I came across another shot of the world's most handsome man," said Elizabeth. "But he was on a date." She gave me a mock frown. "My man is spoken for."

Not to mention living in another decade.

"Well, I'm glad *someone* got to revel in his extensive charms," I said with a laugh. "Don't you wish that guy had a brother, a *much younger* brother?"

Elizabeth held out a photo.

Oh yes, that was him, about the same age as before. How many hearts this guy must have broken in his time… His tight shirt showed off his muscles, and he was looking soulfully into the camera with his arm around…Marguerite.

"How's that for a twist?" Elizabeth asked me with a smile.

"Well, good for her," I murmured. Unexpectedly, I

felt tears prick at my eyes. What a conversation she and I could have had about this gorgeous man. I longed for all the stories I would never hear.

Then Elizabeth directed my eyes toward a long line of photos pinned up to a string above her station. The photos seemed to have been sorted out in groups—of families, I supposed. "The exhibit is really starting to take shape," said Elizabeth.

Feeling melancholy, I missed Gran as I gazed at Elizabeth's arrangement of "Somerset Harbor Families Through the Years." I missed Marguerite.

"It's amazing how many family groups have stuck around in town for decades," said Elizabeth. "Like from Model T's to the present day. Hey, here is one you'll love." She pointed to a photo of a beach scene. A young mother was holding back a grinning toddler, who seemed very anxious to jump into the surf *right then.* He was fiercely holding on to a blown-up inner tube with the face of a purple seahorse. Something about the eyes, the determined look, seemed familiar to me. "Do I know that little boy?" I asked.

"Now he chases bad guys more than he chases waves." Elizabeth gave me a wink.

"Andy!" Which reminded me: I should give him a call.

CHAPTER TEN

"Yes!" Andy said when I proposed again we have drinks out on the porch. "If ever a man needed a gin and tonic, this would be the day."

"Let me guess," I said. "You're back at the Kingfisher to investigate, and craziness has once again ensued involving Max Dakota."

"Half the guests are lining up to check out early from the place. They can't take the noise. The other half is fascinated by the show the guy is putting on."

"What is he doing now?" And was he involved somehow in the murder? He was still way up on my list despite the escapades of Joe and Beth—and despite the new suspicions I had about Elise. A death in the middle of an episode would send Max's ratings through the roof. Was he evil enough to have gone that far for a ratings boost? He was nuts enough for sure.

He was at the top of the ratings still. But a quick internet search revealed *Hauntings on the Delta* was quickly gaining on him. Plus, that show had much more class. I'd watched it a time or two when I sat down with my dinner.

Andy filled me in on the latest. "Now he's got some of the guests involved in his escapades. It's like some kind of circus, Rue. All of these people marching around the lobby of the inn, all of them holding roses and calling for the spirits to make their presence known."

Marguerite's prized roses!

"Max claims he can feel a major rip between the spirit world and the Kingfisher grounds," continued Andy. I could feel the eye roll in his voice. Then he spoke more quietly. "Also, Heather caught the guy going through the stuff Marguerite kept locked up in her desk. Somehow he had a key."

I gasped. "What was he looking for?" This development was huge.

"Apparently the guy is not as stupid as he looks. He won't talk to us without a lawyer present. When Heather caught him in the act, he let out a lot of expletives degrading Marguerite. Said he was only taking what belonged to him."

"Any clue what that might be?"

I interpreted Andy's grunt to be a "no."

"And why is he still there? I thought he had to leave."

"His crew is on notice to pack up or be forcibly removed before the night is through."

"Well, there is that, at least. A little peace for Heather."

We settled on Andy coming by at nine since the store was open late. I told Elizabeth to go on home; she had worked a full day and more. Then I spent the early evening hours catching up on paperwork and helping customers, who came in fairly steadily as the night wore on. I watched as one young woman eagerly snatched up *Where the Crawdads Sing* before continuing to browse. I looked up and smiled as I searched my mental files for books with gorgeous nature writing like the woman's book of choice.

"I loved that book," I said.

"Oh yes, I've already read it," she said with a smile. "This copy's for a gift."

"Unless you have some things in mind, I can suggest more titles with some of the same themes. And some other books in which the beauty of the language kind of draws you in—the way that Owens does."

"It's like poetry the way she writes. Sure. Show me what you've got."

Twenty minutes later, she happily left the store armed with three new books. This week that meant she also got a free canvas tote, suitable for the beach.

I had gotten pretty good at matching customers with books. A lot about a customer could give me hints about what books she might enjoy: snatches of a conversation she might be having on her cell, the slogan on her shirt. That made me a kind of matchmaker extraordinaire between my readers and the rich worlds that existed between the covers of the books we sold. I was always looking out for my customers that way, as my gran had taught me. If they were going to buy one book, Gran liked to explain, why not save themselves a trip and have another waiting when they were finished with book one?

I, of course, enjoyed the extra profits, but I also loved to do my part in enriching people's lives.

Just as I was about to leave for home, I got a text from Andy. "So sorry. Have to cancel. Developments with the case." He added, "Rue, don't ask," as if there was a chance I wouldn't press him hard about said "developments" in the murder of my friend.

I grabbed my purse from beneath the counter, disappointed—and intrigued as well. Since I was too revved up to settle in at home, I made a plan to drop by the Kingfisher after dropping off the pets. Ostensibly, I would be going by to pick up Beasley's asthma meds. In truth, I had enough of the stuff on hand. What I really wanted was to nose around and find out what was up.

If not, I could hopefully find out more from Heather about Max's break-in. Maybe she could tell me too why Joe Ripley was in town and what his story was.

After I parked my car, I had to squeeze through a crowd next to the entrance. Oddly, every person held up a piece of fruit so that it obscured their face.

"Shh!" the voice of Max Dakota hissed at me from behind a cantaloupe. "The clip-clopping of your heels is altering the mood, and the spirits are delicate. The spirits demand *silence* as they make their transitions into the living world." Behind the cantaloupe, his hair stuck out in even more directions than it did on a normal day.

I was infuriated. "This is not a center for your crazy ghost encounters! Nor is it a fruit stand!" I said firmly. *What the heck?* "This, if you haven't noticed, is a dignified and well-respected inn, at which you have overstayed your welcome."

He shoved a kumquat at me. "Hold this in front of you if you insist on speaking. This is a delicate procedure; no faces can be seen. The spirit who has reached out to me today is shy and afraid. In his lifetime, he was hurt." He turned from me to the two cameras that were aimed at him. "As our audience has been informed, a fruit merchant from the eighteenth century is trying to come through."

I shoved the kumquat back at Max with a force. "Well, he has my sympathy. I am like your merchant; I'm trying to get through, and you are in my way."

I noticed the cameras were now turned toward me. "Get those out of my face," I told the men behind them. Then I turned to Max. "Have you no respect? This is a place of business—and a place of mourning too."

As I stomped toward the inn, I heard Max speaking to the cameras in an excited tone. "I hear a message coming through. Not just one spirit, folks, but two. They want to talk to Max Dakota, such a spoooooky guy!"

Heather was watching from the door and rolled her eyes at me. "Isn't it a mess?" she asked. "I was hoping that the cops would have kicked him out by now."

Perhaps they were delayed by the "developments."

"How are you holding up?" I asked.

Her blue eyes were filmed over with fatigue, and her usually neat auburn-colored bun was falling apart into tendrils. "It has been a challenge," she told me quietly, "but things for now are quiet. Well, except for that stuff outside. Would you like some tea? I could use a friend. We could sit out in the lobby, so I could keep an eye out for any guests who might need something from me."

"I would love that, Heather. I've had a day as well."

When we reached the lobby, I settled into one of the white and yellow overstuffed armchairs, part of the elegant period décor Marguerite had put together with such flair. While Heather got the tea, my eyes roved to the wall of photos. Sarah with her cloche and curls seemed to urge me on.

Soon Heather was setting a tray on a coffee table and settling into a chair beside me. "I brought ginger mint. I hope that's okay."

"Perfect." I reached for one of the dainty china cups and poured.

"I had some fruit I could have cut up," Heather said. "But I guess you saw what became of that." She let out a sigh. "The man has been a horror." She leaned closer, lowering her voice. "Apparently, he *yelled* at Marguerite just before she died. Or so the cops have said. He has an alibi, they say, for the time that...*it* occurred. But he made her last days awful—which is unforgivable."

I took a fortifying sip of the warm tea, and my mouth filled up with gingery warm goodness. "The man has no respect. And apparently he thinks that any rules do not apply to him."

"No respect whatsoever. Twice, I've caught him going through the stuff in her desk, and once I even found him in her private room upstairs. Can you believe that, Rue? Looking for something, I suppose, to lure the viewers in. But tonight he will be gone. Bye-bye, Max Dakota!" She poured herself some tea.

Wow. Andy hadn't told me that the office break-in was a repeat offense. Or that he'd been in Marguerite's room as well. There was something that he wanted very badly.

"What did he say when you caught him?"

"It didn't make much sense. Something about how Marguerite should keep her nose in her own business. And he called her such ugly names! I couldn't take it, Rue."

"What did he mean by that? Minding her own business?"

"I have no idea," said Heather. "Kind of ironic, huh? When Max himself was the one in *her* private space, digging through *her* stuff!"

"You told all of this to the cops, I hope?"

"Oh, yeah, I told them everything. They're gonna check her stuff again—to see what he might have wanted." She paused. "He did manage to grab one thing, which the cops took away. He found some kind of letter he was stuffing in a bag when I walked in on him. It was on some kind of letterhead. The letter looked *official*, but I didn't have a chance to see exactly what it was."

I took another sip of tea. "I guess you've heard the

rumors, that Marguerite might have had some plans to leave? I have to tell you, Heather, I was shocked. She never said a word."

"Well, I was surprised—and at the same time, I wasn't. She didn't tell me either, and we were fairly close. A heads-up, I kind of thought, would have been in order, right?" She picked up her teacup. "Of course, who even knows if the rumor's true."

"What is your best guess—yes or no?" I settled back against the deep plush cushion of the chair.

"It wouldn't shock me, to be honest, if she had a plan to leave. She'd been a little...different over the last few weeks. Not in a bad way really. Just not quite as serious. Sometimes...*dreamy* even. Which just wasn't Marguerite."

It was at that point I saw Joe walk through the lobby. He didn't notice me, and he stopped to stare for a long time at the pictures on the wall.

"Who is that?" I asked, trying to sound casual. "He's been here quite a while."

"Yeah, he's been here off and on for about a year. Business or family? I'm not sure. He's a real nice guy, and apparently majorly successful," she told me quietly. "Something to do with tech. I've heard him on the phone with some big-deal people—mover-and-shaker types. The kind who are always in the headlines, if you know what I mean."

I nodded. Our town brought in our fair share of celebrities, but like everybody else, I'd learned to play it cool.

"He grew up close to here, from what I understand," continued Heather. "He and Marguerite liked to talk about the old days in the Harbor, way before our time."

Elise walked up to the desk and firmly rang the bell.

"And then there is that one," Heather said beneath her breath, her face growing dark. "That one is a challenge. Excuse me for a moment."

I watched as Heather made her way to Elise and gave her some brochures. Then Heather returned to her seat as Elise walked out, almost stalking.

"I gave her those same brochures last week," Heather told me quietly. "She just likes to demand things for the sake of pushing us around."

"What is her deal?" I asked.

"Apparently," said Heather, "she works at some museum in Boston as an assistant or whatever. What brought us the displeasure of her company, I have no idea. A very sour sort! At first I thought she might be in town for a funeral, some sort of sad occasion. She arrived last week, and during those first days, she was just distraught." She sighed and poured more tea. "From the very start, she and Marguerite had words. I don't know what was said, but it's the first time in my life I saw Marguerite almost lose it with a guest. But to her credit, Marguerite kept her cool." Heather shook her head and was quiet for a moment. "What with Elise and then Max Dakota, Marguerite's final days were pretty miserable."

We sat awhile in silence. "At least we have the photos," I said to Heather gently as I eyed the wall of pictures. "Elizabeth has come across some photos of Marguerite you'd love. Perhaps you could add them to the wall when the festival is done."

For courage, both of us wandered to the wall to glance at the different versions of our friend smiling at us from the frames.

Then a picture caught my eye—Elizabeth's vintage beau. He was sitting on a cooler, a bottle of beer in his hand, laughing out at me as if to say "Hello! Here I am again."

Heather moved beside me. "I stop by here all the time, to say 'Good night, Marguerite' or 'Good morning' or whatever."

"Who is that? Do you know?" I nodded to the photo of the seventies version of *People Magazine's* Sexiest Man Alive.

Heather laughed. "Oh, it's so funny that you asked.

It's the guy who was just here! That's Joe Ripley, the tech guy, in his younger days. Marguerite told me he was up here on the wall and made it into a little game to see if I could find him." She looked at me and winked. "I have to say he was pretty fine back in the day, you know?"

Hmm. Looking *very* fine. And now Elizabeth could stop by at the inn and see her guy in the flesh. Did I have news for her!

But like Marguerite and Max and Elise and Beth, this man had his secrets.

Which secrets had proved deadly in room 282?

CHAPTER ELEVEN

"None of this makes sense," said Andy as he closed his eyes, frustrated and exhausted. He leaned back in his seat while our lunch sat, half eaten, at the wrought iron table on my porch. "There is no reason in the world," he said, "a man of Joe Ripley's status would resort to theft. In the last year alone, the amount he gave to charity equals *half my salary* for a year. What you tell me doesn't fit."

"And yet there he was." I bit into my turkey on rye. We'd stopped by for takeout after Marguerite's mid-morning services—an event that was jam-packed.

Three rings belonging to Marguerite had been recovered that morning at the pawnshop I had spotted on my alpaca mission.

"Those rings, by the way?" said Andy. *"Twenty-two*

thousand dollars. That's what the things were worth. Do you know what I could do with that kind of money?"

I almost spit out my potato salad. All of that for three little bits of finger sparkle!

The items had been brought in by a woman with what proved to be a fake ID. It was almost surely Beth, which left me and Andy reeling.

Andy slipped a second bite of roast beef to an eager Gatsby, who had always understood Andy was a bigger softie than I would ever be. The more he dealt with criminals, Andy always said, the more he came to prefer the company of dogs and cats. As he munched on a chip, he glanced once more at his cell to check for any updates.

The rings had just been found and matched to Marguerite that morning. Now we waited eagerly to hear what Joe and Beth might say.

"Beth is at the station now," reported Andy, apparently having read the update on his phone. "Joe's whereabouts are unknown at the current time."

Both of them had been present at the services that morning. Beth had been seated with a shockingly feeble-looking Al. When had I had last seen Al? A month or so perhaps.

Joe had been by himself and seemed greatly overcome by the music and the pastor's words. Despite his oddball behavior of the last day or so, his grief seemed genuine to me. And I considered myself to be a perceptive reader of not only books but of faces and reactions.

I found myself a little shocked at *how much* he was grieving. Could it be guilt instead?

"Joe Ripley," I said now, lost in thought as I stared into my coffee. "What's his story, Andy?" I gave up and slipped a piece of cheese to Gatsby, not to be outdone by my guest.

"A widower for three years. He came from a family of some means here in Somerset, but most of his fortune is self-made. By all accounts a brilliant guy."

"So no need to weirdly steal those rings." *Or possibly do worse.*

"We've had our eyes on him, of course. Because of conversations between him and Marguerite that reportedly caused Marguerite to cry not long before her passing. They could have known each other from way back, I suppose. When both of them were young and living here in town."

Oh, they did, I thought.

Andy reached for another chip. "But he seems to have cut all ties with the old hometown until the last year or so, when he started coming back on an intermittent basis." Andy paused to stuff the chip into his mouth and chew. "He seems to be handing off the reins of his company to his number two—little by little, it appears. Slowing down a bit. And taking time to visit some old haunts, I suppose?"

"What's the deal with him and Beth? She probably wasn't *born* back when he lived in town."

"And he never chose to get a room at Captain Jack's. So I would not imagine the two of them were friends."

"Beth." I could hardly catch my breath when I thought about her possible involvement in the murder. But *someone* had been insistent the Kingfisher not be sold to compete with local interests. Insistent enough to slash some tires. How desperate had Beth been to keep Captain Jack's afloat?

"Things are bad for Beth and Al," I said, filling Andy in about the problems with the bank.

Andy raised an eyebrow. "Those are some other facts —very relevant—that we didn't know. I think maybe Bob should give you a job, and this boy can retire."

"No, thank you. Keep your job. I will stick with books." I picked up my last bit of sandwich. "Al looked terrible this morning," I said quietly to Andy.

"Those treatment costs, not to mention all those drugs, have no doubt done a number on whatever they've saved up."

"Treatment costs?" I set my sandwich down. "What kind of treatment costs?"

Andy gave me a sad smile. "Oh, I guess at last the professional detective knows something that you don't." He looked me in the eye. "Al is fighting cancer, has been for a year. Stage four, Rue. It's bad."

In my mind, Al ran energetically down the beach, throwing frisbees with the kids who stayed at Captain Jack's. In my mind I heard his imitations of a pirate that would leave the kids in stitches. Energy personified and a kid's sense of fun; that always had been Al. Did he have a clue what his wife might be doing to…supplement the income from the inn?

"So much heartbreak this week." I pushed away my plate, my appetite now gone. The vibrant reds and yellows of the trees next to the porch seemed out of sync with the day's mood. "So this case, I suppose, will be wrapped up fairly soon," I said. At least there was that.

"This case is an odd one," said Andy with a sigh. "On one hand, you've got Joe and Beth acting really weird—and less than a mile from where the rings were found. And on the other hand, you have that oddball Max Dakota. Joe and Beth might have gotten their hands on the rings, but that fool had the brooch."

Max! In all of the excitement, I'd forgotten the latest about Max. I leaned eagerly toward Andy. "What was in that letter? The one Max took from the inn?"

"Rue, how did you… Oh, just never mind. You seem to have your ways." Andy looked at me and frowned. "You know the drill, of course. I am not at liberty to—"

"Don't even say it, Andy. I have told you stuff—much to your advantage. Now it's your turn; share!" Then I spoke more gently. "You know I'll be discreet." I did understand the pressures of his job.

He sighed. "Marguerite, it seemed, had uncovered information that Max Dakota was a fake."

"Captain Ahab on a boat! That sounds like a motive."

"Of course, anyone with half a brain would know that stuff is fake. But *evidence of fraud* is a whole other thing, and Marguerite found some stuff. Recordings of ghostly whispers hidden in the pockets of the staff. Machines that can project images and lights onto walls and floors. Some other things as well."

"Well, good for her, I say." Leave it to Marguerite not to look the other way. She had always held people to high standards and come down hard on fools; Marguerite spoke her mind. "So she confronted him?" I asked.

"She did, and she wrote letters too—to *Paranormal Hunters*, *TV Addicts*, maybe other sites as well. Max, as you have witnessed, was disrespectful and disruptive to the other guests. Marguerite finally had enough and told the idiot to clean up his act and go—or she would put an end to his charades. When he refused to leave—and carried on even worse than ever—she told him she intended to make good on her threat."

My mind was spinning now as Beasley climbed into my lap.

"So, yeah," continued Andy. "Max snatched a letter from her desk to *Paranormal Hunters*. But what he doesn't know is that it was just a copy. The letters had been sent."

"And shortly after that, Marguerite was dead. Andy, that is huge. Is he in custody right now?"

"He is. We picked him up last night in light of the latest incident. The guy is alibied, but that doesn't mean, of course, he was not involved. He seems more show than action—the type to get somebody else to do his dirty work."

"That creep could have done it. He could have killed Marguerite."

"And we still have the matter of the other missing jewelry. Twelve pieces all in all," said Andy as he checked his phone again. "We checked Max's room, of course. He claims he took the brooch as some kind of 'conduit' to reach out to Marguerite 'beyond the veil.'" Andy rolled his eyes. "They've checked Beth's home and her car. Al's truck, Captain Jack's, Joe's room, all of the places." He took a long gulp of his water, and I noted once again how exhausted he appeared.

We sat awhile in silence, allowing the quiet afternoon to wash over us as we contemplated.

"I've never seen a case like this one," Andy said. "Compelling reasons to suspect not one but three."

"*Two.* I'm almost sure it's two," I said. "Beth might have *stolen* those three rings, but murder? Andy, no." I was feeling shaken. Beasley, as if in sympathy, snuggled closer to me.

"Well, one thing I've come to know in this line of work: you never really know what a person is capable of doing; things are never as they seem." He rubbed at his forehead as if he felt a headache coming on.

"And then there is Elise," I said, "who shows up in town, seemingly with an anger directed at Marguerite. *Jewelry* disappears after Marguerite is strangled. Then in comes Elise to the Seabreeze Bookshop to get books on —are you ready?—selling heirlooms and antiques!"

Andy's eyes grew wide. "You never told me that."

I took a sip of coffee and raised an eyebrow at him. "You've been hard to catch—for more than half a second."

"Guilty as charged," he said. "I'll be so glad when this is through." Then the tiredness in his eyes gave way to a look of calculation. "Elise checked out this morning. But in light of what you say, there's a chance those jewels might be in a car headed north to Boston, where she lives." He let out a sigh. "You know, the hatred she seemed to have for Marguerite was strange. No one can explain it, and Elise did not say much." He reached for his coffee, took a sip, and shook his head. "So now the suspect list is four. It's just uncanny, Rue. With a lot of these types of cases, you go for weeks and weeks with no good suspects at all."

Oliver jumped into my lap as Andy spoke. Beasley looked at Oliver, affronted, then scooted over to make room.

I scratched both cats behind the ears. "Perhaps there was some drama over how the property came to be Marguerite's. I would think the land and the house itself—an Armory Beaumont—would be worth quite a lot."

"*Very* valuable," Andy agreed, confused. "But as far as I can tell, the property and home don't have a thing to do with Elise Montgomery." He peered at me over his coffee cup. "But why do I get the feeling there's something I should know?"

"Oh, there is quite a lot." I gave him a teasing smile. "A little lesson for you: Don't be in such a hurry to get off the phone with your friend Rue. She can just be full of useful information."

"You have made your point," he conceded grumpily. "I am listening, Rue."

"The building and the land were in Elise's family once upon a time if my suspicions are correct," I began. "Because Andy, here's the thing." I proceeded to fill him in on the startling resemblance that Sarah Perkins and Elise had to the Kingfisher "ghost." I explained how Sarah's family had once owned and made their home on the property. "And with the resemblance between her and Elise, I can't help but assume that's Elise's family too."

"Very interesting," he said.

I answered some questions before he stood to go.

"This lunch has added more to my already full to-do list," he told me wearily. "So I suppose it's best I get on with my day."

His phone buzzed after that, and he listened briefly to the caller.

"Be right there. I'm on it," he said, hanging up. Then he turned to me. "Someone has spotted Joe. At the park on Pearson Way, and the guy appears to be despondent." He ran a hand through his hair. "Joe and I had a nice rapport the day I met him at the inn. Ribbed each other some on football. Maybe that will help since we need the guy to talk, and so off I go."

I had met him that day too. Looking frantically for

Beasley, I had chosen Joe to go to for help. Something had drawn me to him: a kindness in his eyes, a look of concern that matched my own despair. But had my radar gone off-kilter and led me to the man who had murdered Marguerite?

Andy's phone went off again, and his expression changed as he listened to the caller. "On my way," he said, a new alertness in his voice.

When he hung up, he sighed. "They've found the missing jewels. Elise Montgomery was stopped on her way out of town. Going almost ninety in a sixty-five-and-over zone. Highly inebriated in the middle of the day—with jewelry in her purse." His voice had taken on the clipped tone of a cop on a mission. "Luckily, she hadn't gotten far; she's still in Somerset. So no football talk for me," he said. "I'm headed to the jail. Two officers are with her now at the traffic stop, about to take her in."

"So it was *her*," I said.

"*Something's* up with her. As well as with the others. Confounding case," he said, halfway out the door.

CHAPTER TWELVE

I reached shakily for a glass of water as my mind reeled from the news. My emotions ping-ponged from confusion to a hot rage toward the snooty woman I'd first seen in my shop.

But my gran had taught me to deflect bad feelings into action. *Joe.* I could go to Joe! Now that Andy couldn't. Perhaps he could help me understand how the puzzle pieces fit.

I gave Elizabeth a call to update her on my schedule. Then I grabbed Gatsby's leash, causing him to let out an excited yip, which meant both "Hooray" and "Would you hurry up?" Then we headed toward the Mayapple Nature Park, which luckily was just a ten-minute walk away on Pearson Street.

I breathed in the crisp fall air, willing it to calm my

nerves. It felt good to stretch my legs and walk off some angst. Soon, Gatsby was straining on his leash as the park came into view. Mayapple Nature Park was one of his happy places.

It didn't take me long to spot Joe on a bench. A weekday afternoon, somewhat overcast, wasn't prime time in the park. Still in the expensive-looking suit he'd worn to the funeral, Joe sat very still with his head in his hands.

I approached him quietly. "Hey, Joe. You okay?"

As before, he looked nervous and a little startled to be caught out by me. Not that mourning in a park made him look suspicious, as his other outings had.

"Rue." He gave me a sad smile. "If you weren't such a lovely woman and me a tired old man, I would almost swear I was being followed."

"I live just down the way. Do you mind if I sit?"

"Oh, no. Not at all. Perhaps a little company is just the thing I need. A man alone with his own thoughts can be dangerous, you know."

As I settled on the bench, Gatsby sat at full attention, staring happily at Joe, almost as if the man were a rare piece of art. That was the way Gatsby looked at people that he liked the best.

"Today a lot of us are hurting," I told Joe quietly. "I think I'm still in shock."

Joe glared down at the ground then stared into my eyes. "Rue, would you tell me this? I always trust the wisdom of someone who loves books. How can one forgive oneself for the…unforgivable?"

I tried to keep my shock from showing on my face. For the love of Jane Eyre, was a *confession* coming?

My heart was pounding in my chest. "Joe, what do you mean?" I asked him breathlessly.

"I mean that I'm a fool."

I kept very quiet as I waited, hoping (and terrified) he would tell me more. Andy had taught me how to keep my mouth shut at a time like this—never, of course, thinking I would really need to know. The two of us had been glued to some true-crime show in which a suspect might—or might not—be about to tell the cops what had really happened during a double homicide.

"You see, this is an example of where they get it wrong," Andy had ranted on that day. "The foolish cops are always rushing in to fill the silence with more questions." He'd leaned back on the couch. "No, no, no, no!" he said to the TV cop. "Let the *suspect* fill the silence when he is good and ready. The information that you need will come from him, not you."

Now, Gatsby moved a little closer, still looking up at Joe, worshipful almost.

"Well, aren't you the handsome boy?" Joe reached out

toward the dog and looked to me for permission. When I nodded yes, he rubbed behind Gatsby's ears, and I saw some of the light return to the eyes of the man. But it was short-lived. He was very quiet before he spoke again. "Heartbreaking day," he said. "Unfair. Just unbearable. All of the adjectives."

I tried to keep my breathing calm and steady. If a confession was to follow, it was taking its sweet time, detouring here and there.

Joe looked up at the colors on the ancient branches that crisscrossed above our heads. Weak sunlight had begun to shine through in bits. "I thought I might find her here." He spoke softly now, as if to himself. "She said I should watch for the chickadees and sparrows, and she would do the same. That way she believed I could keep her close." He closed his eyes. "So are there chickadees in the great beyond where Marguerite has gone?" He rubbed Gatsby's head. "What do you think, boy?"

I didn't understand. "So, when she told you that, she *knew*... Marguerite understood beforehand she was about to die?"

"Oh, please forgive me, dear, for my incoherent ramblings. That was decades back—the day I left this place and headed for New York."

"Oh." I breathed in deeply. "So the two of you were

close…back in the day?" Andy would tell me to be quiet, but that was not my style. Perhaps *nudges* would be fine.

"Love of my life," he answered. "I was fool enough to think that kind of love was easy, that it would come again." He paused. "But, Rue, it did not. That kind of love comes once or sometimes not at all." He stared up at the trees. "Oh, I had a fine life, as did Marguerite. I married a good woman. I've had success in business, seen the world, had friends. It's all been very pleasant…" He trailed off, lost in thought. "But with Marguerite, it could have been a life with *magic*. And I walked away."

Gatsby gave a sympathetic whine and rested his nose in Joe's lap, gazing mournfully at his new friend.

"But you got to have this year," I said, understanding why he must have come, remembering he was now a widower. "You got to have one year of magic."

This man must have been Marguerite's happy secret. What was it she had said?

I think it will surprise you, and it's…well, it's rather nice. That's all you get for now. But when we meet on Tuesday to go over the spreadsheet for the event, you'll get hint number two.

Joe must have been the reason Marguerite had plans to sell. She must have planned to move to be with her old love.

But still. That did not explain the weirdness or the

secrecy between Joe and Beth. Had they really tried to pawn those stolen rings?

I had to keep him talking.

I tried silence for a while, but—forgive me, Andy—the silence didn't work.

"Marguerite seemed different lately, happier," I said. "She promised she would tell me soon what that was all about. Now, I imagine it was you."

"I know the word got out that she planned to sell. We had only recently come to that decision. She wanted to have time to tell her friends in person—over tea and things, make it an occasion. We debated for a while: Somerset Harbor or New York? Then we decided—neither. We'd start over somewhere new like a couple of young kids." He gave me a sad grin. "Destination yet to be decided."

But there was some darkness too in the past that Marguerite had remembered on that day. *I have caused a lot of hurt. Forgetting is a solace, Rue, I do not deserve.*

Now I turned to Joe. "Marguerite had some regrets. Was it over you, the fact she let you go?"

"She blamed herself, it's true, for not insisting that I stay. But I blame only me. The thing is that my parents were all about the money and the status and those unimportant things. We came from money, and she didn't. If they did not find the girl I chose to be 'suitable,' there went all the money for my university. And like a fool, I played along. I thought there'd be another Marguerite out there for me to find one day. But I found out too late there was only one like her."

"She did have deep regrets over something in her past," I said.

"There were some…unfortunate circumstances in her life, some of them early on," he said. "Marguerite, when she opened the Kingfisher, had some plans, you see, for a different kind of inn. Where a portion of the rooms would be set aside, free of charge, for young women in need—much as she had been." He gazed intently at me. "How much did she tell you about her story, Rue?"

"I just knew there was something…a sadness that ran deep."

"She made a promise long ago to herself and Sarah Perkins," Joe continued.

I perked up at the name.

"Sarah was the mother of her best friend at the time," Joe explained. "Marguerite for all intents and purposes grew up in the home of her friend Hetty—with Sarah as a kind of mother to Marguerite as well."

"And the house that she grew up in is now the Kingfisher Inn," I said thoughtfully.

"Marguerite's parents were neglectful and sometimes

lacked the funds for even basic stuff like food and running water. What little money they did have often disappeared down her father's throat in the form of whiskey."

My hand went to my chest, hurting for the younger version of my friend.

"But then there was Sarah. In Sarah's mind, she had *two* daughters. Marguerite was hers just as much as Hetty was. She'd lost some children to an accident when they were very young. She used to say that Marguerite was her 'bonus from the universe' after the universe had beat her up the way it did."

My mind went to Elise, who I was guessing might be a grandchild of Hetty's. "So the property went to Marguerite?" I asked. "What did Hetty think of that?"

"Oh, she was fine with it—at first. Hetty, you have to understand, got some property as well. And hers at one time was worth more than the house and land that went to Marguerite. But then Marguerite's inheritance went way up in value almost right away. And Hetty was resentful. Hetty by that time had moved away, and a kind of coldness grew up between the two of them, which devastated Marguerite."

"Did Marguerite ever hear from Hetty...or from any of her family? That is if Hetty married." I was almost sure the family line had gone on—to include Elise.

"I don't think she ever knew what became of her old friend," said Joe. "But Marguerite found joy in her work at the inn, which in the early days allowed her to give back, which was important to her. For years and years, Marguerite, you see, set aside the second floor as a free, safe space for young girls with no one and nowhere to go." He let out a sigh. "But then finances intervened, and she had to rent the rooms out just to pay the bills." He raised a playful eyebrow. "Although every now and then —although most wouldn't notice—there were women at the inn who didn't pay a dime." He let out a sigh. "Still, she beat herself up all the time over what she saw as a promise left unkept. She felt she did not deserve the nice things she had—fine necklaces and rings and such to suit her exquisite tastes." He stared down at the grass. "But those were gifts, you see. From me. And they came with strict instructions she was not to sell them for the benefit of others." He gave me a wry smile. "I knew her heart too well. Once my business took off, I'd send them for her birthday." Then his eyes went blank. "Just a little bit of sparkle, the least that I could do."

"Those jewels…" I began. His weird behavior near the pawnshop popped into my mind. His deer-caught-in-the-headlight look the day I ran into him at Captain Jack's.

"I know, I know!" His face turned red. "I know

you've seen some things. But Rue, I swear to you, I was only doing what I had to do—for Marguerite." He sighed. "I cannot believe what I resorted to—the fake ID and all. Things got so messed up; *everything* went wrong."

He paused, and I waited. Soon, he began again.

"Just before she died, Marguerite convinced me she had to sell three rings. It was for Beth and Al, who were on the verge of losing Captain Jack's. Then before she could do it, Marguerite was gone. And that, at least, was something I could step in to make right. It was that important to her."

"So you took the rings to Beth?"

"That's what I was doing the day I saw you there. I'd met Beth in the back with the jewelry, hoping my assistance could be a private matter between me and her. And I was just in time it seems. The bank was losing patience. They held off on foreclosing when Beth reassured them she had something—in her hands right then —that she could sell to raise some of the cash." He paused. "I hope this can remain, Rue, between you and me."

"They're proud people, Beth and Al."

"The place might still go under, but not today, it won't. And I plan to help them more—to do that for Marguerite." He looked down at the grass. "At first, it seemed fairly simple. I knew where Marguerite had set the rings aside—in the top drawer of her dresser wrapped up in a scarf. She'd pulled them from the safe for Beth. Then—what a disaster, Rue. A list of *missing jewelry* becomes a crucial part of the death investigation. So we had to be very careful in how we went about raising money with the rings. Thus, the sneaking around and secrecy I know looks really bad. I guess we could have told the cops we had the 'stolen' rings and why. But how bad do you think that would have made us look?"

The man had a point. "Pretty bad, I guess."

I believed what Joe was saying. Gatsby had a better sense of people than I did, and he was currently napping peacefully against Joe's feet. As if I, his owner and best friend, wasn't even there.

We sat awhile in silence, and I wondered what was going on at that very moment with Elise. Had Elise confessed by now? The old fury worked its way back into my chest. Elise must have been the one to accuse my friend of fraud, sending the police chief off on a wrong-way tangent. Just as Marguerite was about to start a new phase of her life.

"Elise Montgomery," I said. "Do you know specifically what she might have said to upset Marguerite?" Perhaps Marguerite had confided in this man from her past, giving him the details about the hurtful conversations.

His face filled with rage. "The woman was a monster. She accused Marguerite of tricking Sarah into giving her the property."

"Was Elise related somehow to Hetty and to Sarah?"

"That would be my guess. Marguerite was closed-mouth about it. I think she was very hurt. But there were a few things that I overheard." His eyes went dark with anger. "Marguerite, as you know, was the last person in the world to commit any kind of fraud. To include her in the will—that was Sarah's choice. With no contingencies at all. And those rooms to be set aside for the unfortunate young women? That idea was Marguerite's—*after* Sarah made the will." He waved his hand in the air, as if shooing off the toxic accusations. "Perhaps that talk began with Hetty, and this Elise was indeed one of her relations. No one will ever know since Hetty long ago broke contact with anyone in town." He let out a long breath. "Marguerite told me that the family still owns the piece of property that went to Hetty in the will. But either she or her descendants rent it out. On Dancing Badger Way."

"I walk past there sometimes with Gatsby. Such a pretty street."

"Cute little white brick house, red door, lots of trees.

Marguerite and I drove by the other day. Seemed to be vacant. Such a shame."

I was glad that in the end my friend had Joe back in her life for drives and companionship. "I felt so bad this week that Marguerite didn't get to tell me what her secret was," I told him thoughtfully. "But now I guess she has. And look!" I pointed to a top branch, where a chickadee was looking down at us.

Joe looked up longingly. "Well, that must be a sign for me to tell you the rest."

"The rest?"

He rubbed his left hand, where I noticed a gold band.

"Right before she died, we did what we should have done all those years ago." His voice grew a little softer. "We lost forty years, Rue, but for one week and two days…Marguerite was my wife."

CHAPTER THIRTEEN

J said goodbye to Joe and was taking in his news when a text came in from Andy. "Elise is gone—escaped!"

I called him right away.

"What?" I cried when he picked up, skipping the "Hello." I knew the man—as he always was— would be short on time.

"Would you believe she just took off in her VW Bug while the officers were talking? Turned their back for just a second and heard the engine start. The woman was just *gone*. It was quite a chase with the perpetrator flooring it and taking crazy turns like a whacked-out fool. I am just amazed that no one was killed. But can you believe *they lost her*? The whole force is looking for her, but she's nowhere to be found."

That's when an idea hit me. "Dancing Badger Way! White house with a red door. Andy, go there now." It was in the family, not currently rented out; it would be the perfect place for Elise to hide.

"Rue, you aren't talking sense. Who in the world lives *there?*"

"No one. Andy, go!"

I would go as well. I gently nudged the napping dog. "Up, up, up," I told Gatsby. "You get an extra walk today."

He perked up at *walk.*

I hurried down the sidewalk, glad Gatsby loved a fast walk as much as he loved a nap. Soon, we made the turn on Dancing Badger Way, where all seemed still and quiet—an ordinary day. Three houses down, I came to the little house matching Joe's description. There was no VW on the street or in the drive, but there was a closed garage. If Elise, as I suspected, was a relative of Hetty's, she might have an opener to get into the garage and slip into the house.

I slowly continued on the walk past one house and then another, all the while listening for the sounds of sirens. Then I turned around. When I passed the house again, I took note of the fact that the windows were all dark. But flashes of color inside caught the light from the sun—sparkling in red and blue and green—as a figure passed a window. That must be Elise—and the missing jewels.

Hurry, Andy. Please.

It wasn't long before three cop cars appeared around the corner with no lights or sirens to warn of their approach. I heard screeching brakes and then the slamming of car doors as five officers, including Bob and Andy, made their way to the house.

Bob glared at the darkened windows and the empty drive. "Just as I suspected, there is no one here."

"She's inside the house," I said, and Gatsby yipped energetically as if to back me up.

"Well, where is the car?" asked Bob. He fixed me with a hard stare, a flash of irritation in his eyes.

"In the garage, I think. I think someone in her family owns this house."

Andy watched me, open-mouthed, as if to ask "Where did that come from?"

"I see no signs at all that anyone is here," said Bob, not convinced.

I turned back to the house. "Oh, I beg to differ," I calmly told the chief. "Someone's at the window now!"

Elise was staring at us, her eyes wide with fear.

How moronic can she be? I thought. Anyone should know that *looking out a window* could kind of blow your cover *with the cops right there outside.*

"It's her!" a young cop shouted, and things moved quickly after that.

A blur of blue rushed toward the door, and soon Elise was being led out with one man on either side. Her face was now more red than its normal ghostly pale.

"The only thing I took was what was coming to me!" she yelled at one of her captors. "That woman stole from me—stole from my grandmother! She was the crook, not me! I tried to reason with her. It didn't have to end with anybody dead if she had only listened."

Gatsby strained against his leash, barking angrily at her.

Andy was the one to slap handcuffs on Elise. "We are arresting you," he said, "for the strangulation death of Marguerite May. You have the right to…" The rest of his words faded out as I bent to calm Gatsby down.

The men headed to their cars, and one of them helped Elise into a back seat.

Bringing up the rear, Andy paused to nod at me. "I don't know how you do it, but…well, good job, Detective Rue." He gave me a wink.

"So it was really her." Finally, I could breathe.

"Appears to be," he said. "Now off to the station for a little chat."

"Let me know how it goes," I said before I looked

down at Gatsby. "Come on, boy!" I said, feeling lighter now. "Let's go sell some books."

CHAPTER FOURTEEN

 little less than two weeks after the arrest, I sipped on a martini, watching crowds pour over the exhibits. Many of the festival attendees carried bags with purchases; the merchants would be pleased.

"Great event," said Bill Bright, stepping up beside me. "Fine idea we had."

We?

The idea he'd referred to as "wasteful frippery"?

But I just let it go. The weather was too perfect, the attendance too astounding for me to be anything but glad. Above me, twinkling lights were strewn across the soaring branches of an elm.

"Things have turned out well," I said.

The whole town seemed to be in a mood to find comfort in each other after a tragic chapter in the community. Elise—who was indeed a grandchild of Hetty—had given more details to police about the strangulation and the events that led up to it. After she was questioned, Andy had dropped by at the bookstore to fill me in on the missing pieces.

It was a dark and twisted picture Andy painted for me as I listened in the comfy reading nook over a cup of tea.

Hetty's resentment of Marguerite, it seemed, had grown into family lore. An especially deep hatred had simmered in the mind of Elise, the most hot-headed and unbalanced of Hetty's three grandchildren. Elise was the one who looked the most like her great-grandmother, Sarah Perkins. But in temperament, she matched Sarah least. As she read articles about the success of the inn and its famous "ghost," Elise imagined all the money her family had missed out on through the years, having no idea Marguerite sometimes struggled to keep finances in the black.

Elise had tried and failed at a number of careers and eventually set her sights on a prestigious architectural-urban design program. To her surprise, she was accepted. This was finally her chance, but she lacked the funds. Her hatred of Marguerite at that point reached a peak, and she vowed to get the funds she felt were hers by right. Upon arrival at the inn, she had explained to

Marguerite her connection to the Perkins family and demanded money for tuition—or else she would "expose" the owner of the inn as a "charlatan and fraud."

Marguerite had been visibly upset, not out of any sense of having cheated Hetty but over the reminder of her former friend, who once had been so dear. Elise had further upset Marguerite with talk of Hetty's recent death—and the bitterness with which Hetty often spoke regarding Marguerite. As if to prove a point, she had haughtily asked Marguerite how many rooms had been set aside that evening for those who were in need.

When Marguerite refused to write a check for Elise's first year of tuition, Elise had decided she would get the funds any way she could. She carefully watched Marguerite's activities until she finally caught her at the safe, which was in a little alcove outside room 282. Elise had seen the jewelry Marguerite proudly wore, and she suspected it could bring a hefty price.

On the morning she pounced on Marguerite and grabbed the jewels, the struggle had moved into the vacant "haunted" room, whose doors were open at the time. Luckily for Elise, no one was around to see. The guests who weren't at breakfast were outside, glued to Max Dakota's latest antics in the garden.

Later, as rumors spread about the sale of the Kingfisher, Elise was the one who sent the threats to

Beckham Properties. By then police were asking questions about the brash encounters she'd had with Marguerite. Best to deflect attention onto someone else, make it appear that Marguerite was killed by a competitor and not a disgruntled guest.

Now, as I watched the activities around me, I wished Marguerite had lived to see this day. I tried to banish my dark thoughts and to think instead of the soft jazz coming from the band in the back corner of the garden.

I saw Beth coming toward us, but she looked away as she passed me and Bill.

"Fine event," Bill called, forcing her to stop.

"It will do," she said, nodding solemnly to me. "We'll get used to the change, although the old October Days worked for years and years. Tradition has its place as well."

Overhearing her, Brenda walked up to our group and gave me a side hug. "Rue has given us an amazing gift with Martinis in the Garden," she declared. "I for one appreciate it."

Beth stared down at the grass. "You are, of course, correct. Rue, I apologize. It's been…well, things have been difficult this week. A whole lot going on."

My eyes moved to Al, sitting proudly with his driftwood art but noticeably weak and frail, even more so than at the funeral.

"I hear raves about the food." Beth said it with a smile, but her eyes looked sad. "I was just heading to concessions."

"Grand idea," I said. "I was heading there myself. Why don't you go back to Al, and I'll bring the two of you some Italian sausage rolls. I hear those are divine."

"And Marguerite's cheese straws." Heather appeared to my left. "All her recipes, thank goodness, were right there in a drawer—all of them handwritten. Mine don't taste the same, but I think I did okay. They're in those little bags with different-colored ribbons over at table two."

I headed toward the food, stopping to watch a crowd of children at the Encounter with Alpacas. Buttercup's watchful eyes seemed to hold a question about why her old friend Rue had not come by to say hi. Never one to hurt an alpaca's feelings, I headed over to the favorite spot at the festival. Buttercup stuck her head out to me through her sea of fans, greeting me with the wet-tongued enthusiasm I remembered from before.

"They love you, Buttercup," I told her with a laugh. "I knew you'd be a star."

Moving on, I glanced at Elizabeth's exhibit, stopping at a photo that showed Marguerite arm in arm with Sarah. Perfect for the theme of "Families Through the Years." I wondered if anyone would notice that one detail of the photo was quite remarkable. Would they see that there she was—our town's famous "ghost"—standing next to Marguerite?

Other photos in the group showed Marguerite with her other "family"—her friends from the town. There were photos, too, of Marguerite with Joe: peddling bicycles, huddled with groups of friends, sitting on a stone wall with his jacket wrapped around her carefully against the wind.

From across the lawn, Joe gave me a wink, knowing I would keep his secret. Marguerite, he'd said, had wanted to be careful how she explained to friends the reason for her marriage and her plans to leave. Now, there was no need to explain at all.

"The best day of my life will be a precious secret between her and me," he'd said. "Well, between her and me and *you*," he had added with a smile. "Thank you for our talk. It did me a lot of good."

Proceeds from the sale of the Kingfisher and the recovered jewels would be used to help young women who needed a hand up, as outlined in the will. A foundation would result—Heirlooms for Heroines. And it would hopefully keep going through donations from the public through the years.

"I hope you'll serve on the board," said Joe, who had been named executor. "She thought a lot of you."

"I'd be honored," I had replied.

Now, Joe was deep in conversation with Elizabeth. I watched for a while, amused, from across the lawn. My best friend, normally so reserved in a crowd, now looked downright giddy. And why would she not be? The vintage "hot guy" from her dive back into the seventies was right beside her in the flesh, a corn dog in his hand.

Then I stood in line for food and shortly after that began to make my way to Beth and Al. I took in the happy crowd and the twinkling lights. The air smelled wonderfully of gardenias and fried foods.

We did good, Marguerite.

I could almost hear her answer.

Just exquisite, she would say.

Brenda appeared beside me to assist with the trays of food and drink. "By the way," she asked, "how is Erin doing? I'm available to help!"

Erin? Did I know an Erin?

Brenda laughed at my blank expression. "Your *cousin* Erin, silly!"

"Oh! *Big family* of cousins! Very, very big. Erin—yes, of course." *Sheesh.* "Erin's great; she's well. Found a lovely place to purchase in Vermont."

"Oh, you should visit soon."

I decided on the spot I would do just that: visit Vermont, of course, not the non-existent Erin.

"A vacation! Great idea," I told Brenda with a smile. "I could use some time away. Vermont, here comes Rue!"

# # #

Thank you for reading! Want to help out?

Reviews are a crucial for independent authors like me, so if you enjoyed my book, **please consider leaving a review today**.

Thank you!

Penny Brooke

Penny Brooke has been reading mysteries as long as she can remember. When not penning her own stories, she enjoys spending time at the beach, sailing, volunteering, crocheting, and cozying up with a good book. She lives with her husband and their spunky miniature schnauzer, Lexi, and two rescued felines, George and Weezy.